A GOTHIC SOUL

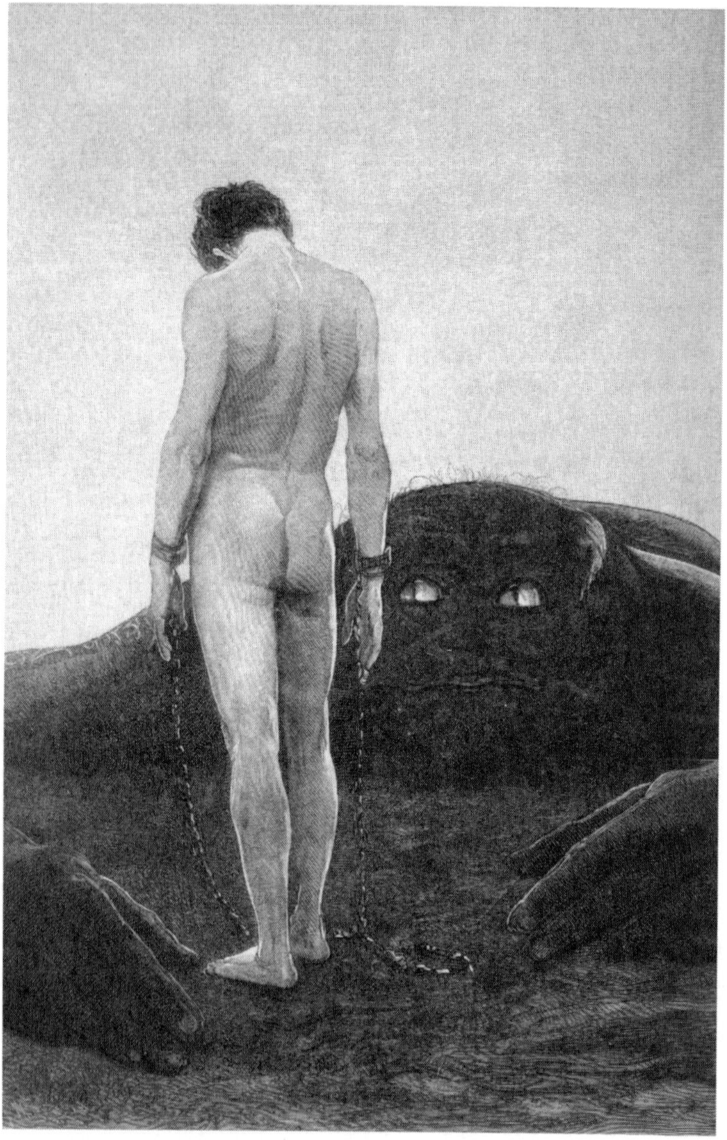

Jiří Karásek ze Lvovic

A GOTHIC SOUL

Translated from the Czech by Kirsten Lodge

Artwork by Sascha Schneider

TWISTED SPOON PRESS

PRAGUE

2025

ISBN: 978-80-88628-12-5 (SOFTCOVER)
ISBN: 978-80-86264-91-2 (E-BOOK)

CONTENTS

AUTHOR'S PREFACE

A Gothic Soul is not a novel in the usual sense of the word: it is a diary of emotions and moods, of the undulating play of the spiritual world, an account of *stories of the soul,* of everything that agitates the inner self beneath the waves of nuances, fragrances, and tremors with which the real world inundates it. The chimera of a daydreamer who wants to inebriate himself with life and around whom *the dream of life* flutters constantly like a veil that cannot be removed, and *who believes that for life it is necessary for that dream to come true,* and the tragedy of this delusion — that is the inner story of my work.

It has almost no plot. The protagonist merely walks around his room, or wanders the streets and reflects. A nameless protagonist — without external tribulations, subject to no outside calamities. He has become separate from everything real and material. Rather than plot, a series of stories and episodes, you will find the *painting of a soul,* uninterrupted by plot details — a continuous flow, *a spiritual stream.*

My book is not a narrative; I have composed it from spiritual processes. Impression follows impression. Feeling gives way to feeling. Spiritual states are in constant agitation. The melancholy of an empty childhood yields to the melancholy of youth, which feels that life fails to fill the void of days. In addition: melancholy from the impossibility of eliciting a response, the futile search for a friend — that is another source of suffering. The impossibility of faith — another. Skepticism about the Czech nation — yet another.

Suffering from the impossibility of fixing ever-shifting life in a set form — that is the real protagonist of my work, the shades that I evoke, with which I animate the stage. Spirits step forth from the dark background, they meet, they merge, they separate, and their phantasmagoria, the play of their nuances, the oppression of their dusks — these are the lines and forms from which I have composed *A Gothic Soul*.

The character whose story I tell does not exist in reality. Life clamors around him but brings him neither joy nor torment.

My hero is insensitive to the suffering that real life could cause him. The true suffering is in his soul, and while he seems not to feel real suffering, he is unsettled all the more by "fictional suffering," to use an expression of Flaubert's — suffering created not by reality but by his inner self, and which he observes in grievous terror, with a pallid, strained countenance, gazing into his own soul as though hypnotized by its bottomless, mysterious depths.

Fear of himself — that is what pushes the hero to escape from himself, to flee from himself, that is what spurs him on and shatters his peace of mind, and *the impossibility of escaping himself* is what destroys him. This psychological problem of *A Gothic Soul* replaces the plot and storyline found in other novels.

A Gothic Soul is something else as well: an autobiography in which melancholy youth confesses its sorrows and its hopelessness. It is also a document of the times — not contrived, which is always tasteless, but spontaneous, which sometimes has its charm.

Biographies are abominable: they relate insignificant details about significant people. Only autobiographies are tolerable, and only when they disdain reality. For autobiographies offer so many opportunities to portray the soul, and so much freedom to ignore reality and to create a work of art from one's own life.

A Gothic Soul originated in the diary of a twenty-year-old, and nonetheless it has been treated as something artificial, intellectualized, and labored.

When it was published, the hero was said to be abnormal, pathological. Admittedly. *A Gothic Soul* does not follow the paths of the commonplace, the everyday. Does this make it less true? It has been forgotten that some may feel almost the same anxiety when confronted by the normal as others feel when confronted by the abnormal. When will critics here understand that the purpose of art is not to limit itself to the vulgar, the average, and the common, that its concerns should be with everything save "respectable sobriety," as Goncourt rather caustically put it — tedious banality, which realism has tried to make the exclusive source of artistic inspiration?

It was a good thing that realism did not describe reality "as such," that it made banality even more banal and vulgarity even more vulgar, and was thus at least somewhat interesting. Henri Céard's *Une belle journée,* I believe, is the culmination of what this genre can achieve. Yet why do people think that art that stirs the author's soul is less truthful than art that leaves it completely cold? Why is it that only the author who describes things as they are is considered truthful and not one who believes the poet stands between things and their mystery rather than before them?

Reality has only one purpose in art: the artist must become familiar with it so as to know how to avoid it. He should learn from it so as to know how to distance himself from it.

To say that art should represent the world as it really is would be to assert that the purpose of art is to imitate those things that do not interest us even in reality.

Realism has asserted as much, but in so doing it has merely concealed its artistic impotence. By proclaiming that art has no other purpose than to portray what exists, it hides its inability to accomplish anything beyond that reality.

Zola ridiculed Sand for her particular fondness for portraying actions that had never happened to her and for describing people she had never seen. He thus paid a great compliment to her imagination and a small compliment to his own inventiveness. What he forgot, however, is that if art were simply to mirror reality, then either art or reality would be superfluous.

The truth of a work of art is its congruence with our inner dream, and not with external, real facts. Art should enrich life, not impoverish it, revealing it in the cold light of sober knowledge: it should make life more miraculous through the eyes of those who see in its mundane forms the traces of another, more beautiful imaginary world.

The artist should not impoverish his own sensibility or

deprive the world of its intriguing iridescent colors just because sobriety proclaims them to be illusory; he should strengthen and impassion his character, and he should experience all of his follies just as powerfully as his suffering. For only his emotional experience will be present in his work, whereas everything that derives from his life in reality will vanish into the darkness from which nothing returns.

Fiction is eternal; reality perishes. Invented forms live; real ones vanish. Truth is ephemeral; illusion, everlasting. Passions and emotions experienced in real life never have the same force as invented passions and emotions: how many times is Hamlet's melancholy revived in us, even though we will never again feel a sorrow once felt? The real thus becomes unreal.

Where are the love and friendship we once felt? They did not last even a single lifetime. Those we once loved madly still live, yet now we pass them by with indifference, whereas Francesca da Rimini and Paolo never cease loving one another, perhaps because their love was never so passionate in reality.

What, then, is the sense of adopting forms from life when they perish so quickly?

When Rossetti's belovèd Elizabeth Siddal died, he placed a manuscript of his poems praising her beauty into her coffin, under her golden locks. This was not logical. Elizabeth was too real to remain, and the poems were too fictional to perish with her. Understanding his error in time, Rossetti opened the grave to retrieve the poems. Poor Elizabeth! What a ghastly skeleton grinned up at her horrified lover! But her beauty and fragrance were preserved in his poems. And the poet saw that everything he had dreamed was an illusion: Elizabeth could not be his muse if she had turned into something so hideous. His muse was in his *inner self.* He was his own inspiration.

Let us not be mistaken: no one can inspire an artist when he bears everything within himself. Rossetti only thought he was inspired, while in fact he gave of his own beauty, not the beauty of a Sheffield cutler's daughter.

There is a moral in this story for those who bind the evanescent names of people whose love is transitory to works that are to outlive them. One melancholy evening they experience Rossetti's horror upon opening Elizabeth's coffin: they find the corpse of someone they once loved, but the work remains as alive and wounded as bleeding roses plucked that very evening...

Do you understand this symbol? Real love disappears, while imaginary love is eternal. *Beata Beatrix* lived in Rossetti's soul, to which Miss Siddal could never gain access.

And real suffering is more transient than fictional suffering. Whoever has once despaired and ripped all the joy from life, like a withered branch from a tree, will still have reason to smile in time, but no smile will ever grace the lips of the hopeless Ophelia.

Life is deaf to us, for it is as devoid of emotion as nature: only art created by great individuals, our brothers, is able to convey a secret to our soul.

Let us, then, not be afraid to forget life for art, for only its beautiful lips may tell us the truth of all of our being.

I

He was the last scion of a venerable chivalric family, of which a few impoverished women remained, afflicted by hysteria, while several other family members had died of madness.

He often thought about hereditary degeneration. And he often wondered whether the shades that lay plotting in his soul were the same shades that had haunted his relatives who had died of madness.

The gaze of one particular relative frightened him terribly.

He had died of religious mania, quite young.

He had hung the cousin's portrait over his desk.

The older he grew, the more convinced he became that they resembled one another. But he thought his senses might be deceiving him — until a relative he hadn't seen for some time shrieked at their resemblance and plunged him back into doubt.

The dead man, whose eyes, face, mouth, and hands were his own, was returning to the family. They had the same blood, the same desires. And when he became dangerously ill, he suppressed the restless yearning for life in his heart. He wanted to die, for he was afraid of inheriting his dead cousin's madness ...

But he didn't die.

He arose from bed even paler than before. The sound of his voice was more somber. He looked even more terrifying.

His eyes now disturbed anyone who looked into them. They lacked luster. They harbored a secret that seemed accusatory, though it could never be expressed in words.

He did not seek anyone to confide in, as though he did not have enough time for intimacy. He always seemed to be at death's door. He observed everything with a long, fixed stare, but his eyes did not see things, as though they did not even have the time to perceive contours. It was as though his soul should leave without any memory of this world. Everything that could even distantly link it with others should remain foreign to it.

Still, nobody was gentler, nobody prepared for life with more care, nobody endeavored to step more silently to solicit mercy from death.

He lived like this from one day to the next.

People walked past him, and he walked past people. His lips did not dare to question, even with the utmost diffidence.

Although he was convinced of the invisibility of his burden, he was still sometimes frightened by the thought that he might be found guilty. He feared giving himself away unwittingly, and that some involuntary movement would betray him.

At the same time, he was tormented by the consciousness that in living this way he was acting against himself. He was alienating his own soul, opposing it to a cold, calculated life with a mask of indifference.

He yearned to encounter another being between life and death with a mysticism that would bring resolution to his nameless secret, and empower both his soul and his body. *And he*

wanted to relate to that being in the same way as he related to himself.

He wanted to be a priest.

A monk. Yes — a monk . . .

Remote monasteries and old churches stimulated his imagination. A strange style: Gothic, later redone as Baroque architecture. A Baroque altar, and above it a painting by Rubens or Škréta. Everywhere a musty odor. And paintings on the ceiling. Above the altar, glass coffins. In them, embalmed corpses. Full of gold that had lost its luster. Silver that was inertly dull. Delicate silk, ash-white or with a pinkish hue, like human skin. Faces so severe and eternally unchanging . . .

He would live in that church. And during Mass, in the closed choir from which he could see nothing but the altar, he would kneel and pray.

Then he would fall silent and listen to the believers praying. Unfamiliar people. Their voices would resound darkly through the thick grating. Petitioners he would never see.

He would live in the monastery . . . ten, twenty years? He didn't know. He would not count the hours, the days, the years. He would not know what was going on outside. Perhaps wars would break out . . . plagues would rage. No, he wouldn't know about anything. The townspeople would be dying out. But every day he would kneel in the choir in the same way and piously pray in the same way. He would listen attentively to the voices of the believers below — until he heard a strange noise. Not praying, but sighing. The voices are so weak. He senses misfortune. He peers anxiously through the grating. Yet he sees nothing. Are there wars? Epidemics? No . . . no. What is it to him?

Bowing submissively, he would whisper a prayer. And as quietly as ever he would go back to his cell through the sacral corridor, long and silent . . .

At that time the company of people was more intolerable to him than ever. The repulsion toward them that had been building inside him was now surfacing uncontrollably.

Everything of this world irritated him: people, their gestures, houses, sidewalks, the sky, animals, plants, everything that was intimate with life and to which the traces of people clung.

He dreamed of something more meaningful than the most profound things of this world. And those people and those things were penetrating his secret. It was as though they understood everything . . . They were laughing at him.

In profound melancholy, he heard a voice speaking in his inner self so pervasively that he could not silence it. He ran from church to church, unsettled to the point of madness. He threw himself down before crucifixes. He fantasized over tombstones. He exhorted miraculous statues of Mary adorned with gems. He lifted his gaze to choirs and galleries. He lowered it to flagstones. He immersed it in a deluge of gilding and painting.

He crept up and down holy staircases. He beat his chest before monstrances, before the Host. He kissed the bronze ring that Saint Wenceslas had clutched before his murder. For hours his stare was fixed on the plaques in the wall, on the painting in the narrow window, on the old reliquary.

He wandered all of Prague, all of its churches. He did not speak a word with a living creature for months. He spoke only with dead things in churches, chapels, crypts, and cloisters. He felt that his soul had suddenly found itself in their magic circle. He joined his life with them. He bound it to their mystical influence.

At first it was all but incomprehensible to him. He could breathe only air that was laden with the scent of incense. He wished to see no other faces but the faces of the dead. Images of saints captivated him. And, irritated by living plants, he found pleasure in the artificial chlorotic flowers of the altars.

Everything he experienced in the world outside was dry and empty.

Standing before the mystery of the altar, he felt himself coming back to life. The mist had dispersed and clarity came to his soul.

Lazarus in his first life, in the world outside, was unconscious and confused. But one day, when his soul was dead to him, Christ said in a soft voice: "Rise and walk!" And Lazarus was as though resurrected. His soul knew everything.

Christ walked before him. He would follow the bloody footprints of His agonizing steps.

Could there still be some illusion in this life? He had submitted completely to His will. He had given Him everything: fear, uncertainty, humility, body, sin. Now he could kneel peacefully before the tabernacle, listening to the fierce, eternal gale sweeping through the world. He would no longer be alarmed by the silence of the neighboring chamber, rustling in the fire, the groaning of stairs, the reflection of a mysterious light. Now he knew that only He and his own soul were present.

He would lay his head on His soft lap like a sick child, so

slowly, and surrender to fate. Then all the angels would descend from heaven and gather to protect him and watch over him as he slept. In that great love of mysterious beings his exhausted soul would have respite. He would feel their burning hands and breathe in the fragrance of their trailing vestments, their pink lips, their flowing hair.

It was an illusion. He saw that he was trying to live a life completely lacking in naturalness. He assessed his life. He yearned for certain impressions, colors, incense, gloom, ecstasy. But they did not invigorate him; instead, his health deteriorated.

He had created a Gothic soul for himself. He wanted to live in the Middle Ages for a few hours. He wanted to share the medieval conception of life. Yet it was an illusion. The Middle Ages were dead. The lives people had lived then could no longer be shared.

He felt a chill in his soul. He was in despair.

Above, high up in the choir, a voice was singing an old hymn. What was the lone singer singing about, what hopes?

It was so dark in the church. Even the candles on the altar seemed to be going out.

The voice trailed off and echoed like a gentle lament of hopelessness. It was the voice of someone who had withdrawn from the world forever and descended into the grave alive. At that moment horror sliced through his soul.

Who demands such a sacrifice? An abyss seemed to open before him. He peered through the grating of the choir. But it was dark there. The singer's voice had suddenly fallen silent. Everything was dead again.

Now he could no longer forget the voice, which had said: all is vanity. He stared at the altar painting, at the sharp contours of the saint, at his gaunt, ascetic face, into his extinguished eyes that said: all is vanity.

He stifled a cry. He wanted to stand. But he was rooted to the spot. He moved only his hand. His lips were frozen in a whisper: all is vanity . . .

II

He remembered his father and mother only indistinctly. And he didn't even know whether his present image of his deceased parents corresponded, even if only approximately, to the lost reality, the bygone days of his youth.

He was brought up in the care of his elderly aunts in the ancient family home, full of dark, heavy furniture, surrounded by the traditions and legends of the generations that had lived there for entire centuries.

In its hallways he sometimes saw his father's shade return to life.

Thin, spindly, jaundiced, his father would walk around with sluggish steps, always clad in black. He behaved distrustfully and coldly to everyone with whom he spoke. He was a recluse. He suffered from a persecution complex. He dulled his senses with morphine. Toward the end of his life he would not leave his room at all. All the windows had to be covered. Sunlight brought on anxiety attacks.

He preferred to imagine his mother full of a white, delicate beauty, like a saint with a golden mystical radiance just darkening over her hair, a gentle, visionary woman, her tresses, face, hands, bosom, everything exuding a subtle fragrance, etched in lines of an all but unreal delicacy, in an unearthly magic, imbued with suffering.

The atmosphere in which he was raised was painfully withering, an atmosphere of indifferent grays and gloomy browns.

He drifted among them day after day as from one stain to another, arrayed on the image of Apathy and Spleen.

For entire days he would wander from chamber to chamber. He would stare out the windows, where along the wet walks the stream of what is called life slowly flowed in the ceaseless, dank drizzle.

He was entirely absorbed in his thoughts. When addressed, he gave the impression of one who has just been awakened from sleep. All of his movements seemed automatic. His responses, preferably limited to one word, revealed that his brain did not wish to overexert itself.

He never displayed curiosity. Things in themselves did not hold his interest. He never said that he loved one thing, or hated another, or that he wanted this, or didn't want that.

He grew up anemically pallid, wasted rather than thin, and he looked lifeless. Only his eyes, ice cold and colorless as glass, sometimes overcame his apathy. Then his gaze was long and willfully piercing. He would discomfit whomever he looked at, for it seemed as though he wanted to penetrate all of the mysteries of that person's being...

After the death of his parents, the boy fell into the hands of his relatives, the old, spinster sisters of his father. His upbringing continued in an atmosphere of scapularies, images of saints, and rosaries. It was the beginning of pilgrimages, visits to cloisters, and endless prayers.

Whereas his body lived mechanically, in his soul another world was born and grew. Everything that left him indifferent or repelled him in the real world now seemed to take on greater life in the most intense hues.

That mystical ability of his soul transformed the emptiest room, full of torpid dead air, into a chamber full of beauty and splendor. Everything in it would suddenly flare up and begin to glitter. He would see the phantoms of beautiful people, whom he would dress in the golden and silk garments of the princes and princesses of children's fairy tales, and they would nod to him and smile at him.

It was like that with everything.

The ticking of a clock would become the voice of a man telling him in the diffuse light of dusk about furtive intrigues. He would stand up involuntarily, horrified.

The frame of an old family portrait he was looking at suddenly disappeared. Before him stood a living being, with whom he spoke of things about which he had never asked real people.

Everything dead came alive for him, while everything alive died before entering his soul. In a heavy, fantastically carved wardrobe he suddenly saw the doors of an enormous hall, which opened in his mind's eye. And he saw a crowd of people in the most impossible attire emerge from it.

The protruding stones of the corridor turned into tombstones in his mind. He imagined a huge crypt beneath it, where the dead rise and look around, astonished. A fly striking the windowpane would soon become not a fly, but a mysterious hand warning him that he would shortly receive an unexpected visit.

Most of all an ancient curtain hanging at the entrance to the bedchamber stimulated his fantasy. It was embroidered with a pattern of golden birds with outspread wings on a faded blue background. They flew diagonally upward from the bottom, and their flight seemed to continue into the infinite. When the curtain moved, in the sudden tremulous flash of the gold embroidery the birds seemed to come alive and flap their wings in preparation for powerful flight.

He had many secret relations with those birds. Each one of them had its name and its tale.

At other times he would dream he was in a garden full of mysterious flowers. How many colors, and what fragrances! Wondrous roses, tulips, garnet-red flowers, and irises with the scent of myrrh! Bloody poppies like red lips, so soft and delicate! He had never seen such splendors before. What rich clusters of hot calyces, as red as illuminated rubies! And what green grass, more luminous than emeralds!

His soul wandered the gardens and greedily gathered the blazing splendor of the flowers into heavy bouquets. He bathed his hands in their sensuous, fragrant breath. His daydreams would always suddenly spill out into the most indeterminate areas.

Then there would no longer be a discrete garden, a discrete fragrance, discrete hues. There would be only the single hum of it all — colors, hues, fragrances, brilliance — everything all together. It was something exciting, something that captivated his entire being and gave him pleasure, but again not a real pleasure — merely something that gripped his throat and kept him from crying out, at once tormenting and sweet.

Thus his soul transformed and exaggerated everything on which his eyes fell. He used it all to create a completely new world for himself. His pleasures and cares were not the pleasures and cares of the people around him, but his very own pleasures and cares.

He lived with the mystery of all things. He loved to give himself up to mystical dreaming.

His soul was not of this world. The church in which he prayed was not of this world. It was far away, indeterminately far away. It was "beyond this world."

III

Upon reaching maturity, he was delivered to some extent from the familial yoke. Yet his overall circumstances did not change. His aunts had decided his fate: he was destined to enter the clergy, and the whole of his education was focused on that goal.

He began to live a double life. In one life, aloof, seemingly foreign, he was a rather apathetic young man, entirely obedient to his aunts' plans for him. He went to churches and monasteries with the priest serving as his religious mentor, listened to lengthy discourses in which he could have no interest, kissed his aunts' hands and the hands of priests, and diligently studied the lessons assigned to him.

In addition to this life he led another, which he carefully

concealed from everyone. It was a life of doubts and fantastic phantoms.

Sometimes he would be overwhelmed by such melancholy that he would weep in secret without even knowing why. Then he would give himself over again to extraordinary hopes. It was as though everything in the world had an alluring magic for him. He knew that at some point a life of beautiful dreams and beautiful reality would begin, a golden, exquisite life like a work of art, a proud jewel, covered with precious stones. That was his goal. He would go through life with a smile, with a silent tread. He would be gracious toward everyone. Everyone would be gracious toward him. Everything he touched would be beautiful. And everything he looked at would be exquisite.

He would approach God. Like an irresistible invasion of light, God's mercy would penetrate his soul. Then the moment of the miracle would arrive. He would understand that he was in an extraordinary world in which he shared the company of God. He would participate eternally in the beauty that is concealed from everyone else.

He observed people around him, their lives, and they seemed to him creatures of an entirely different sort.

No one felt so deeply how much beauty there is in dedicating oneself exclusively to dreams. These others had all devoted themselves to something else. How abhorrent they all were with their interests! They assessed everything so soberly. They laughed so insensitively at many things he was passionately committed to. What loneliness!

He was terribly unhappy whenever he found himself in a large crowd. He was unable to pray in church when it was full of people. Not a single pious thought would move his soul. His eyes would wander along the altars, the light of the candles, the colorful petals of the flowers, the lace of the altar coverlet, the sheen of the monstrance. Those were dead things, on which the eyes of all the other people gazed soberly. He looked with them. Why did they come here, why did they clasp their hands here, pray and sing? It was superfluous ceremony. Nobody heard them . . .

It was different, though, when he was alone. Everything came alive. Things took on new forms. They acquired meaning. Everything spoke to him.

He was convinced that only he understood the life of things. No one else understood that language, because their ability to comprehend was so vulgar. That's why no one understood him either. He did not dare confide his inner life to anyone. He knew that instead of understanding he would meet with cold derision.

He was terrified of people. He was afraid of their faces, which seemed to be laughing at him. He expected sneers from their lips. Their hands touched him ironically. And most of all he feared their eyes. They were so prying. They examined everything. They penetrated into everything.

He defended himself from them, but in vain. They kept penetrating deeper, until they saw everything — everything that he did not want to show them, that he wanted to glow only in the crystalline shimmer of his solitude.

He avoided people. Not for anything would he enter a place where he thought there would be a throng. He did not understand how people could enjoy concerts and the theater. They were pressed together, almost cheek to cheek, breathing each other's breath.

He fled the public entirely. He didn't even attend funerals. He preferred to visit solitary graves. He was especially afraid of people he didn't know. He suspected all of them to be enemies. He armed himself with the most inaccessible coldness. He resisted intimacy, which threatened danger. With all of his strength he fought against the mysterious enemy rising against him in the soul of anyone who came near. He desperately resisted the penetrating element that was trying to attack his inner self.

He was still in thrall to the desire to find a being who would understand him, but this was a dream being, and he fled into dreams when the iciness of solitude made him too cold. He conceived this being in the likeness of people he had encountered during the day. But its inner makeup was completely different.

He would speak with it as he never spoke with anyone living. He attributed to it all of the feelings that were stirred up within his own soul.

His soul was always populated with phantoms, which he nourished from reality. His imagination dressed them in the most glamorous clothing and gave them the most gracious smiles.

Sometimes he became so engrossed in his dreams it was as if he had met the object of all his longing: he had found a friend. But it only took one word from the lips of this imagined friend for the illusion to shatter. A single movement would remind him of reality, in which his dream was impossible.

In an instant his friend would turn back into a stranger.

IV

Sometimes his expectations would flag. He came across a sentence in Pascal that profoundly disturbed him: "The purpose of life is not to find happiness, but to seek it."

To seek, to seek eternally! Never to find! What torture!

He studied the old Church Fathers. For days on end he applied himself to medieval theology. But how arid was the desert of theology, its tendentiousness, all of its formalism! It exuded more the atmosphere of a spiritual barracks than a church. He no longer wished to be a monk or a priest.

The word — the most beautiful instrument of mutual understanding with God — how it had fallen to such wretched craftsmanship! It had no spirit. Thoughtlessly they turned it inside out and played with it aimlessly. That was theology, the art of playing with words, exegesis — but the spirit was disgraced . . . A waft of cold air came from everything . . .

It was all logic and reasoning that debased rather than elevated the soul. Did not Satan, speaking to Jesus Christ, pronounce the terrible words: "I am cold itself"? Did not St. Bridget say in a rapture of somewhat misplaced familiarity: "I am He who does not love"?

He sought love and warmth. He did not want to be indifferent and aloof. He wanted to blaze up and burn.

He felt how he was changing: he was losing trust in everything. It was as though someone had removed his soul from his body. His carnality scraped along entirely mechanically. Having wanted to get close to everything, he was suddenly restrained by dogma: this is the path you must take. In the unsteadiness of everything he wished to build a life by the force of his own will. He wanted to acquire virtue through experience. But dogma told him: you must go against sin . . . otherwise you will be lost to Satan. He had to be a slave to the rules, to form, even though his soul yearned to look around the world and choose for itself what his heart desired.

He despised the "model of life for everyone" to which dogma limited him. He did not want to creep up to God with the silent tread of a humble petitioner. He wanted to approach His throne with proud steps, standing tall through all the obstacles, through fear and faith, defiance and respect, sin and virtue. He did not want to go to Him via the convenient paths of moral prescripts thought up by others. He wanted to hack his way to Him through the dense forests of his own dark anxieties. He wanted to feel Him out for himself in the Silence of All.

He fled the church, where the echo of the voice of St. Paul still trembled, turning the living word of Christ into a dead system, transforming the warmth of His love into the ice of dogma. As though drunk on the balmy fragrances of the flowers of St. Francis, he wanted to enter the garden of His love, inflamed with feeling.

He set off down the road, but he did not get much past the border. He disappeared somewhere among the villages of Bavaria and stayed there a whole year, forgotten amidst the woods and the mountains . . .

A year later he returned to Prague, resolved to live by nothing but his dreams.

V

He refurbished the family home to live in and arranged for his solitude not to be disturbed. Among the old walls covered with old-fashioned fabric and wallpaper, from which the gloomy portraits stared down, among the furniture all huddled together against the walls as though in fear, he began to dream about the life he had been unable to live, about its alluring mystery.

To live . . . resounded in his soul. To live for himself . . . To secretly take advantage of all that life offers. To live in the vast silence of everything as in the church of his own soul . . .

To be alone, alone . . .

Once again he was at the door to the labyrinth he had stopped and turned away from once before to head elsewhere . . .

Solitude, cold, the grave. Shades, grief, asceticism. A Gothic soul. Somber, torpid Münster, gloomy spiritual Temple, secluded Fortress, the Middle Ages, something so surly and inexorable . . .

He had fled from that, and to it he must not return.

To go alone meant to mortify himself. To sever all ties with the world. There was a fatal delusion in that . . .

To renounce ghastly, grinning phantoms, not to seek "the pleasure of terror, of horror," but to seek beauty, the harmony of life: that is salvation.

He dreamed in a chamber asleep in the shadow of the blue silk curtains drawn on both windows. Fatigue weighed heavily upon him.

Everything seemed oppressed. He did not think. He did not

feel. He was aware only of the swaying, hypnotic sound of the clock. It seemed to diffuse drowsy, gloomy dreaming throughout the entire chamber. Everything within him was falling asleep. Colors grew softer. Contours merged. A heavy languor numbed his nerves.

The silence mounted from the dismal chamber.

The air outside trembled as though in flames. A faint breeze that had made its way into the chamber blew through a half-drawn curtain, flapping like the canvas sail of a ship. (He imagined a boat asleep on the water in the noontime heat, rocked by the monotony of waves.)

And he sensed the faint smell of wood warmed by the hot weather.

Forgotten fragrances came back to life, dissolved like memories, rained from vases where flowers were drying up, wafted down from the open wardrobe, respired from the open drawer, straggled along the surfaces of the furniture, fled from the folds of the curtains, from the old wallpaper, hung on the darkened portraits, thickened around the gilded chandelier with its partly melted wax candles.

The small home altar with the reliquary in the corner exuded incense from the shabby deep red chasuble thrown over it, and the weapons between the portraits of ancestors in the attire of the Revolution reeked of mold. A stale odor of musk had accumulated over the collection of polished perfume bottles, and the Meissen porcelain with its pattern of tiny roses had the same scent that had clung to it since his childhood.

Odors were in the carpets and the sofa covers, in the scattered pillows, everywhere: odors not of the present, but of the past. A bluish twilight trickled into the chamber, seemingly filled with the dance of whirling dust by the window, above a groove of gleaming metal, spilling in as the curtain permitted, and further playing only in reflections. Deeper in the chamber there were only slumbering, blurred colors — the indistinct colorlessness of everything in a single hue.

He loved the fragrances flowing through the familial rooms. And he multiplied them, filling vases with flowers and leaving them until they'd wilted.

He could dream over roses for entire hours and become inebriated with the colorful hues of small leaves weighed down by a brilliant rose, and tiny, delicate leaves, so light it seemed as though they were made from faded pink or yellow silk, and leaves that were somber in shadow and full of mysterious glitter in light, and open flowers, unfolded, and chaste ones, enclosing in their calyx the secret of their fragrances.

He stupefied his senses with their intoxicating ambergris, exuded from each leaf, from each calyx.

He loved tuberoses most of all. Sometimes he would gather them in every corner of the room and dream as the tuberoses exhaled their heady scent. Sorrowful and sickly tuberoses, snowy white petals that seemed to live only to mortify. As pale as the forehead of a dying man, enfeebled in their flaccidity, vanquished by their own breath, mournful, sanctified by death, bereft of smile, the gaze both of a fully unfolded flower and one still half-closed in the incipient beauty of its pallor.

And all of them, as from beautiful open lips, respired the same pungent perfume, which welled up and mingled with the headiness of the air, filling the entire space, and in it he would dream about the sweet and painless death of the depressed and listless in an agony no longer aware of anything.

He loved fragrances that were sharp, sickly, and pungent, which tormented him. As if he were always being absorbed into them. They would fill his entire being . . . He felt faint from this mad whim, from this mania culminating in such final consequences. Their conquering force repelled everything. Only the fragrances rose, reveled, broke through, and aroused him.

Afterward entire planes of color, oppressive and stupefying, would become fixed in his mind: pink from the roses, faint purple from the hyacinths, and white from the tuberoses and the jasmine — then it all merged in a fit of dizziness in which everything was gone but a desire to forget everything . . . In the illness that afflicted his senses, in the debauchery dulling his being, he was sometimes overcome by the fear that one day the fragrances might no longer affect him . . .

VI

Night had fallen. He was standing on Hradčany before the cloister of the Barnabites. He sensed a dull humming in the lane down which deposed kings had walked. There was a deathly stillness in the windows of the cloister. The house of the dead towered like a somber fortress.

Did anyone still live there? No one knew. Did one of those women about whom no one knew if she was mortified or just unhappy still live here? If so, she certainly did not look like anyone from this world. Her face bore the expression of the solemn resolve of those who are dying of their own accord.

Life here was nothing more than a conversation with oneself. They wandered the walled corridors as though impelled by the mysterious power of sleepwalking. Pitiful eyes, fated to see nothing! Lips, destined to address no one but imminent death! While the soul is astonished at so many trifles in life, the renunciation of which seems a great sacrifice, the house of the dead greets it with the majestic nothingness of all. Nothing . . . that is the essence of everything that eludes understanding.

He groaned, repeating the sentence . . . A faint echo, immeasurably enfeebled, seemed to resonate from the reticent walls of the tragic house, shrouded in mystery.

So someone does still live here. This was her response. The last woman, who will die in her cell with no one to bury her, had answered him from her tomb. She was still brave enough to give a sign of life . . .

The wretched woman.

Lamentable beyond all imagination.

But why wretched? Why lamentable?

He recalled a biblical expression: to flee from Judea to the mountains. To the distant, high mountains. To surround yourself with solitude. To isolate the dream. To have nothing dearer than your own inner self. What a life . . . his lips repeated . . .

To conquer bodily desires . . . To immerse yourself in melancholy over your own inner self . . . To find a continuous but delicate trembling in the agitation of the nerves.

Yes, to find faith in yourself again . . . That is the main thing. For the drama is in us, and in us it must be resolved . . . To extinguish all colors, forget all faces, cover your life with oblivion as time covers ancient statues with moss, to see nothing but dusk and always the same gray wall, so that nothing external diverts your contemplation. Not to distinguish night from day . . .

He saw the faces of ascetic saints, emaciated from fasting, their tragically pallid hands like the hands of those who had long been dead, touching nothing but the crucifix, the scapulary, and the font of holy water. The beauty of their life was to live a single life. To live in a single thought, a single emotion. Not like him, with his life shattered into ten, twenty lives . . . To live a life of contemplation and then, immediately afterward, ennui, then agitated emotion, then daily life. Monasticism — that was the only way to live life in a unified way, to keep one's sensibility completely for oneself.

But to renounce the experience of the world?

It's not easy. To renounce experience — what an opportunity to feel his strength, to have his urges roused! This was the magic of asceticism the world did not understand. Above the experiences we never exhaust, to have an illusion that satiates us — that was the entire secret of reclusion.

Then another memory surfaced.

Last year, on the day of Saint Teresa, he had wandered into the Church of the Barnabites at evening. On that day an invisible hand opened the gates to the cloister.

The church was decorated for the ecclesiastical solemnities. Everything was prepared for the ceremonies. Priests and believers came. Yet no one saw even the shadow of the cloister's mysterious inhabitants. The opaque grating was lowered before the entrance to the cloister. Curtains concealed both choirs. Everything seemed to have died out . . .

Nothing was accessible from the cloister but the altar. Though invisible, the nuns attended divine services. Nobody knew behind which curtain they were kneeling, or how many remained, for they had been dying off for some time.

He was standing behind the last pew in the church. Twilight was beginning in the low windows above. In the church below it was dark. Only the main altar, covered with lit candles beneath the painting of St. Teresa prostrate in fervent devotion before Christ, glowed like a huge pyramid of lights melted into golden mercury, shone like an enormous *castrum doloris*...

The believers' responsory mingled with the Marian litany accompanied by the organ. A stifling atmosphere reminiscent of the Passion, something like the oppressive atmosphere of annual funeral ceremonies, was diffused throughout the church. The flowers on the altars were withering, exuding a grievously somber, cadaverous scent.

The murmur of the assembly seemed to grow. But an increasingly sepulchral silence reigned over the cloister. Then everyone rose and began to sing *Te deum*. The high-pitched voice of a bell from the altar began to accompany the singing, then the voice of the bells in the tower joined in, pealing like a death-knell. In the tragic, suffocating darkness of the church everything was like an attack of that multitude on all of the gratings and curtains separating the inhabitants of the cloister from the people. He listened anxiously for a voice from this voluntary tomb. He heard nothing. They had cut themselves off from the world forever...

A huge naked Christ gleamed white from the crucifix into the darkness of the church, as though conveying a secret command of silence to those who had renounced everything for Him . . . His bleeding wounds glimmered in the dark like a glowing mystical sign, blinding those who did not wish to stain their purity from the moment they beheld the mysterious, holy reflection.

His soul was lost in fantastic dreaming. Figures composed of distorted and deformed contours came into his mind. It seemed as if he were looking through the thick grating. He saw hectic effusions, arms raised and suddenly falling again, figures writhing on the ground. He seemed to see eyes blazing monstrously, eyes that had been extinguished for everything earthly. He saw desperate gestures and postures displaying the awkwardness we associate with the sudden movements of reanimated corpses, yet not a single sob broke the deathly reticence of the lips, which had vowed eternal silence. It was a terrible cry of silence that struggled toward him from the thick grating by the altar. Eternally deadening silence had been laid down as a command on every exigency of life, in the belief that it would drown out the restlessness of the soul by cutting off all contact with the world . . .

But one may never go back. Never. His soul trembled . . . The lights would be extinguished; the visitors would leave. And again the terrible silence of the tomb would spread here, everywhere the very steps of Eternity would be heard. The mysterious inhabitants would again wander the empty corridors between the windows and the doors, always closed, for a whole year . . .

Mad kisses on holy wood! Bloodless, pallid lips pressed against the countenance of the heavenly Lover! It seemed their breath would catch in their throats. Would they finally be heard? The hallucinating senses churned feverishly.

Whose kisses burned on those thin, pallid lips, and whose breath fanned the sunken face? Bosoms lifted with long-awaited ecstasy. Eyes burst into a blaze of frenzied pleasure. A penitent crawled on her knees to the huge Crucifix. Her hands pressed against His sacred Nudity. In a holy convulsion she threw herself on the bosom of the Crucified One.

Her heart beat on the stone breast. And the stone heart, animated by a sudden miracle, shuddered, each beat strong enough to count. A stream of blood reanimated the dead body. She felt the veins tense and the Sufferer's flesh tremble. In pain mingled with pleasure the penitent's body collapsed, unconscious, onto the cold floor . . .

It was night again when she awakened. Again Christ was something Alien, Distant, and again the penitent went to Him, mortifying her naked body, endlessly repeating His Name . . .

The madness of not being with Him and in Him eternally, the terrible curse of creatures doomed to live on the earth!

Eternal night within the cruel walls of the cloister, a night of sighs and lamentation, febrile dreams! God! How impatient You make the soul! To live one more day! A whole series of days! To continue to remain near life!

To hear a faint response from the distance! Memories . . . but terrible! The image of childhood, Mother's face. A lover, the scent of his hair, his hands, his smile . . . no . . . everything has vanished.

The day she realized the emptiness of life, when everything

had become a disappointment to her, she experienced an awakening. But wasn't everything here, too, a delusion?

What a whirl of thoughts can overtake you! Part of her sinful life was still with her. It still had not been mortified within her. Lord, how difficult are Your paths for legs that are too weak!

God, it is still not possible to serve only You. What should she do to desire only You?

God of supreme love, why have You wounded her with such great madness? You do not let her live, that the great gift of Your generosity should fall again from her weak hands!

Like Your servant, Teresa of Jesus, she sighs to You, O Savior, Heart, Purity: why does she have to suffer these torments?

You see she wants nothing but You . . . Why then have You imprisoned her soul in that body?

Extinguish forever her eyes, which have looked upon the sin of the world. Grant her eyes that will see only Your glory. Make her lips mute for the world. Teach her to speak the language in which You and the angels in Heaven sing *hosanna*. And put her heart on the fire of Your love as on the burning coal of incense. God, God have mercy!

Thus he prayed before the altar in the dying gold of the candles and the exhalation of sickly flower petals, scenting the air as though with the odors of plague and hospitals.

He now had the soul of one of the hysterical women huddled behind the grating. At that instant he was unable to do anything but pray.

The believers were leaving the church. The candles on the altar were feebly guttering.

Afterward only a few lights were burning in the poor small chandelier, a few candles whose pallor quivered on the dull surface of the imitation crystal and silver. The church was returning once again to its appearance of a somber tomb, to a frigid night of timid shadows.

The old paintings over the altar darkened faintly. Their colors receded. The animation of their faces and postures vanished.

The great white Christ on the crucifix was turning livid. An indistinct saint beneath the choir, enclosed in a tight old frame of about a shoulder's width, wearing a flowing black garment and terrifying the viewer with the glare and cadaverous face of a man dead for centuries, fell entirely into obscurity. Only his pale countenance, framed with thick hair and whiskers, could still be distinguished as a light stain in the darkness.

Is that Christ? John the Baptist? It was impossible to tell. How strange that manhood was, having matured in vain. It seemed as though the gaze of women who have foresworn all human endeavor, the last kisses of their lips and desirous sighs of their bosoms, had been fixated on Him forever.

He was one of the last to remain in the church. They were already about to shut the doors.

He looked around the church once more. Only now had it returned to its true appearance, as it was perceived by the mysterious inhabitants of the cloister when one of them would creep in here at night. The walls, towering to a dizzying height, gave the impression of the stark and dismal darkness of a prison. The shadows clinging to them looked like graveyard cypresses and thujas. The stiff rows of pews loomed like tombs.

It was like a cemetery here, where the Past comes down at midnight with memories as though accompanying a great funeral procession.

Everything suffocated and oppressed him . . . Lamenting and beating one's head against the ground was all that could be done here. It was impossible to meditate and pray.

The altars rose like formless funerary catafalques. The likenesses of saints on their sides in tortured poses, with their arms raised and their legs twisted upward, with angular waves of stone robes, gave the impression of people afflicted by sudden despair.

And the livid Christ on the cross seemed now to be leaning forward from his instrument of torture as though he wished to descend and flee. Afterward everything merged into a single horror and a suddenly petrified madness . . .

VII

He left the church.

Where he wandered after that, he could no longer remember.

Today everything that had occupied his soul back then was revived. He knew he would not be able to escape the dank tomb of the past into which he had descended, to free himself from the enchanted circle of overwrought blood and nerves in which he had unexpectedly become entrapped. For this atmosphere could not be approached without incurring punishment.

As soon as he did approach, those things ceased to be dead. A deceptive trembling was resurrected in their morbidly mute sorrow. He felt subject to the furtive influence of mysterious relations and a mysterious fatefulness.

He was not alone. Shadows populated his solitude. He no longer spoke to himself. In amazement his lips addressed apparitions that no one had ever seen before.

He could no longer give himself over freely to dreaming as he had until then. *He had to stay vigilant. He was no longer his own master. He was subject to these beings, not knowing whether they would bring him freedom or destruction . . .*

Once again he began to spend hours of hopeless disquietude before the portrait of his relative who had died of religious mania. Once again he began to doubt: didn't his facial features resemble the portrait, didn't his eyes have the same enfeebled sheen of the dead man's eyes?

He wished only for a sign that this was the case . . . Then he would make an end of everything.

His life was so peculiar, yet he could not read a destiny in his own face. Nor could any of the things surrounding him provide him with any profound certainty. They did not reveal to him the mystery of that hidden fold of his being.

There was nothing to do but continue to grope and to seek in the darkness, in a corner of which lurked a monster, preparing to pounce. He wanted to make an instantaneous, unassailable decision right at that moment. We shall be vigilant, his lips repeated.

Night had fallen . . . He was still standing in front of the cloister of the Barnabites. Yes, everything lay in this: to flee from Judea to the mountains, his lips repeated again. To flee to the distant, high mountains . . . to escape forever. And above all to escape from himself.

Some words cannot be spoken, just as in sleep there are

movements that cannot be performed. This was the discourse he now held with himself.

He sought in all things the emotive and potent affinity they had to his being. He did not want to make a single movement until he knew what mysterious force and invisible power reigned in every vibration of his life . . .

Every impression immediately evaporated.

He surrendered to the magic of the poetry wafting from the long-forgotten, moribund cloister, its walls having long wished to make him their prisoner.

He fled far from them, toward life. It was impossible now to return to asceticism. The great glitter of life should dazzle him. Crystal, flashes of silver, music, the bustle of society, laughter, jokes. The dance of life, where he should at least be a spectator, if not a participant.

But everything was so distant. He was sick — he felt it. He could find no peace. It was as though all the atoms of his soul had been vaporized. He could no longer calm himself. He longed for a friend, a kindred soul. How beautiful to give himself to someone and feel that he had given himself to someone. His life would immediately acquire meaning. What happiness! What charm!

He dreamed of a future friend.

He imagined him so beautiful and sad. He would have to be gentle, with fragrant, undulating hair the color of gold. And he would have to have delicate hands: long, pale fingers, as though enervated.

He saw them folded in his lap, moving nervously and then immediately resting again. Their nakedness, their refined whiteness, would arouse him. A delicate, sensuous trembling would have to animate them, and they could not lose their brilliance even in the shadows; beautiful old rings with varicolored stones would have to adorn them, large rings with diamonds, turquoise, chrysoprase.

His voice would have to be colored by grief, so he would seem absorbed in absent and remote thoughts.

The dreams of his friend were so realistic it seemed that someone was leaning toward him, that the breath of someone's lips was mingling with his own. Elated by the being leaning toward him, he lost focus. He saw nothing but eyes veiled by long lashes, as though immersed in shadows, trembling, dark red lips, with flesh as luxurious and fragrant as potent roses just gathered from the bush. In the dizziness that shattered his strength he yearned for nothing but someone to love, who could make him forget about everything that tormented him.

Yes, yes, he should have a friend . . . He should have someone who would look inside him and understand him.

This hope, by turns desperate and suddenly triumphant, took possession of him.

To share with someone everything that animated him, and everything that could not be expressed in words, in a look, through gestures.

To share with a friend the secret world of the soul that requires no explanation. It spills over from one loving soul to another as they draw closer, through a vibration of sympathy. Corporeality falls away like a useless garment, and one soul looks into another, naked, simply, devoid of any obstacles. At such times we feel the person standing beside us is closer to us than we are to ourselves. His being is enriched by our own soul, and we are only a part of what we love . . .

No, he must not languish in solitude any longer.

Yet the friend he longed for did not exist, and he was so immersed in sorrow he could speak to no one.

Everything hurt. In every face he thought he read derision. His nerves felt like the ends of glowing wires.

He resented the lyricism of his soul, its yearning to yield. A soul so torpid and gray, a long, monotonous plain, above it a lowering cloud. That was his soul. Everything so bare and flat.

VIII

He felt he had never experienced youth, so light and alive. Youth fragile and slender, with lips full of the rosy joy of a flower just budding, with the faintly moist excitement of animated eyes, a touch of madness in a young man's movements. Youth, delicate and downy like a sweet memory. As fragrant as one who is uncomforted, filling one's entire being with the breath of smiling luxury rising from the soul as smoke from a censer.

Many times he would have been glad to fill the void of his own life with the reflection of others' happiness; he would have forgotten everything that lay in wait for him in the dark until he was alone again — that terrible sorrow, as if he were leaving his own "I" and observing its isolation.

Everything would immediately become different. The shadows would dissolve. Something more colorful, more vital would shine through his solitude.

He was granted nothing.

INRI

What a life: to see the same faces for whole months, to know beforehand what each day would bring, and to know the answers before the questions were even asked . . .

The light of his life was starting to gutter out before it had even begun to burn. His torments lengthened like shadows in the setting sun.

A cold and alienating void trembled through his soul, and he seemed incapable of mustering the courage to wrench out the dead sorrow. Grief was sinking into his darkened soul without his being able to prevent it. It was soaking into his inner self like twilight into a landscape.

He was overwhelmed by a bitter rush of melancholy, a powerful consciousness of the *nothingness* of life, that everything had lost all value for him. Everything seemed so useless, given the fact that one day his life would no longer be. The thought that he would then slowly rot, turn into nothing, made it impossible now for him even to think about how to make his life *pleasant* . . . The thought blew away all hopes, as the wind blows away dry leaves.

He had comprehended everything; there was nothing anywhere that aroused his curiosity. There was nothing left to do but die. Everything had become bitter, abhorrent. Like the pendulum of a clock he went from point to point, from boredom to disgust, from disgust to boredom. What could he do? What could he grasp onto? All is vanity.

He laughed bitterly. He was conscious of reality. A rocky, harsh road — and one leaves it only for emptiness.

IX

His thoughts now often turned to what connected him to his surroundings. He sought the explanation of his impotence in his being Czech. Was his spiritual world Czech at all? He thought in German and French. He was interested in the French and German peoples. He felt, breathed, and lived in German and French.

No, no — that was a pose. Is everything having to do with the Czech element really so wretched? Poor fields. Stunted crops. Weeds. Sands, endless sands. Would he really never hear a voice from out there, a really moving, human voice that would rouse his heart, speak to him from the plain? Not even the slightest *sob* of oppressed life?

This was too cruel to be true. Yet it happens that we discount at evening something too cruel to believe, only to discover the next morning that it is indeed true.

Truly nothing. Dead, eternally dead.

That was the hopeless truth. Everyone was imprisoned here as in a house whose inhabitants had all died. Every endeavor was crushed here.

Dead, dead, he repeated. He felt the futility of every pursuit. Regret overwhelmed him. It was no use living if everything was to perish.

He was deeply moved by the imminent demise of all things. Yes, now everything was clear to him. Prague was animated for the last time by an element that had something in common with the long extinct nation that once inhabited it . . . It was not the nation reviving, only its fiction . . . this element's existence would be rather brief. How petty all of the nation's trivial struggles, feeble protests against the vast numerical superiority of the predatory element assailing it with enormous force! How meek the sentimentality with which this people clung to the glorious purples of the past and watched over the crowns of the ancient kings, rotted away long ago! Nothing belonged to it — except inexorable death.

The hypnosis of that death enthralled him. A strange feeling overcame him — as though everything around him had already died out, and he too was but a part of that death. Yet everything seemed to have been leveled out by death. He walked solemnly along the cobblestones of dead Prague. It seemed to him that eternity itself was wandering here through the dust of decomposition. The Czech nation and everything related to it was now something so sacred it could only be loved. Yes, everything the nation had demonstrated in the centuries of its existence was now pure and respectable.

The odyssey of the Czech soul. Her errant paths, her debilitating efforts to attain not power, but truth . . . That was her history before catastrophe struck. Bent over a Bible in a solitary cottage, she sat by a timid lamp and humbly waited for the instructions of truth, for its revelation. She wanted to draw truth from her own depths as if from a secret well. Waiting: that was her symbol.

The words she spoke appeared inane to others. She spoke with shades that descended into a broad and spacious land swept by northern winds. She spoke, hoped, and waited, until nobody was listening to her any longer. She raised her eyes to the heavens. Everything earthly became smoke for her. She freed herself from the baseness of everything that reeked of corporeality. She wanted to transform everything into the beauty of intimate thoughts, but everything dropped from her weary hands.

Even when her waiting had come to nothing, as her enemies bound her hand and foot, she continued to hope and call upon providence. There was so much inexpressible tragedy in her disillusionment. The enemy became fixed and rigid above her and allowed her to awaken from her languor for a moment. In her last breath she still adored the truth she did not live to see, the beauty she never savored, and the light that never reached her.

Then she died in her fetters. Everything that destiny had frustrated, everything great that could not be born in this land, veiled the dead Czech soul, the most wretched of all wretched souls, in shadow.

The more the Czech nation and Czechness itself lost its contours in his thoughts, and the more everything became legendary, the more glorious that unfulfilled mission appeared to him. Everyone here should kneel and weep. The profound mysticism this people exuded! Hus — no, he was more a theologian. But Chelčický! And Comenius! What depth, what a sea! And this people had died out, not exhausted from luxuriating in debauchery like other nations, but from the struggle to find truth. It had died from the harshness of fate, from a tragedy that wrenched its heart . . .

He awakened from his dream. No, it was not the end of everything. Around him he heard Czech being spoken, the streets bustled with life whose surface, at least, was Czech. Suddenly he felt so cold, alienated from the present. He felt not the least attachment. He was simply indifferent to the everyday life passing before his eyes. What a difference compared to the fever which, just a short while ago, had him in the grips of the struggle of the perishing Czech nation against merciless destiny!

Overcome by regret, he lamented everything. Life, the vanity of his land, the impossibility of finding a friend, the utter misery of his fate.

There was no one he could love. Everything left him indifferent. He stared at everything apathetically. There was nothing that could even at least provoke him. He loved life and people as long as they remained abstractions for him. But when he came close to them, they did not gratify him. They irritated him. His illness became unbearable.

I am wounded, he repeated. I am bleeding, and I will bleed to death.

I yearn for the impossible. I am dying of the possible. This is my sickness. It is called the inability to breathe. I am suffocating. The air that surrounds me is not for my lungs. I will waste away. I will lose myself in myself. I will disappear. Nothing of me will remain. Everything I dream about will come to nothing. Even my tears will leave no traces. My tears, too, fall into a wasteland . . .

A phantom is standing over me. An oppressive curse. It had to be . . . Still — a desperate question: must everything perish like this . . . every endeavor . . . only because it is born in this ill-fated land, doomed to extinction?

He was from a cowardly caste, which had felt a foreign boot on its back for several centuries . . . That was his Czechness . . .

Nihilism, yes, nihilism is the only philosophy possible for this people. Nihilism, the morality of the slave, the philosophy of pariahs. Whereas pride and aggression seethe in the blood of other nations, the one prevailing emotion in this degenerate race: cowardice, and with it an absolute distrust of everything, life above all . . .

Nihilism. It shatters everything, every endeavor. It bends upraised heads. It makes outstretched arms fall, desires run dry. What strives for the heights soon falls. And what begins to fall is already lost.

What nothingness was hidden beneath the surface of *that kind* of miserable existence . . . Hour after hour passes. One is no longer aware of their senseless inanity. Yes, the hope might be cultivated at times that one could possibly even breathe in this atmosphere. One might have hope in himself, in his strength, in the future. Maybe even believe every now and then in the fertility of this atmosphere just because it is Czech. And it never occurs to him that every future day will be like every day that has already passed, and that nothing will ever be accomplished here, precisely because he is in Bohemia . . .

He was despondent. He was quite aware that surely today he would part anew with the sole phantasm in his life. As with religion, the principle of nationality was beginning to seem an anachronism.

All logical deductions notwithstanding, his soul wished to divorce itself violently from that principle to which all ties had yet to be severed. This was why he was so depressed; this was the cause of his anxiety and pain. Unlike the religious principle, the national principle had yet to *overcome itself*. It could only be overcome by the gradual over-intensification of nationalism, which would lead to broadening that substratum called humanity. There had never been enough nationalism here. This nation had so far only lived out in full its religious feeling, and thus the religious principle could be overcome. Yet in its Czechness, in its nationalism, it had still lived too little.

How he wavered, how restless he was! He desired faith. But faith was dead. Belief was no longer possible. He yearned for gratification in intimate contact with the world. But the cold of solitude was all he felt. He yearned to live his Czechness to the full, but all the paths he had thus far taken led him away from national sentiment. *Would he at least live his humanity to the full?* Would he reconcile the improbabilities of his soul? Or would he spend his life yearning for love while filled only with hate? Would he wish to fill his days with work while making only frustrated, futile attempts to do so?

He felt illness overtaking him as he raved about health. It approached him furtively, with steps distinctly calculating and crafty. Where could he go to escape? How could he overcome these contradictions?

His enigmatic, mysterious eyes became moist with melancholy shadows. He saw himself go toward the infinite, unsatisfied, seeking and not finding. Later he would no longer seek or yearn. He would not even ask: who am I? Where am I going? This would be the last harbor of his life. Nihilism . . .

X

He wandered up to the top of Petřín Hill and looked down at the city. It gave him only a mixed impression of indefinite, noisy space. An immense fatigue descended from everything. Everything seemed so futile to him, as the colorful diffused into the colorless, the bright into the dark, light into shadows . . . He stood for a long time without thinking, his gaze fixed . . .

Suddenly he was disturbed by someone, perhaps a lover of solitude like himself, sitting down on a nearby bench.

They looked at one another instinctively, as if something had immediately drawn them to one another. No words passed between them. And they didn't even dare to gaze at each other a second time.

Yet from that moment he felt himself to be under the magnetic power of the newcomer. Was this someone who could be his friend?

Ah, to live, just to live . . . Everything, just not this miserable existence, this half-life. Nothing whole. Nothing proper. Not even proper passion, proper feeling — not even proper boredom. Just quasi-feeling, quasi-passion, quasi-boredom. Someone smiles, he smiles back, without even knowing why. Someone says: come with me, and he goes, and does not even know why or where he is going. That's all. And that's life. What is it all for? All this foolishness, all this torment for unrealizable chimeras!

A ray of the setting sun stirred up golden dust in the air. Then it faded, and twilight veiled all forms. Orange shadows were falling on the pantile roofs, in the old courtyards, and in the gardens full of blossoming hawthorn.

At once he looked into the stranger's eyes. He had never seen such eyes before. In the darkness their green hue turned into a soft, indolent, yellowish amber shade, as though burning with warmth, which seemed to absorb and imbibe the darkness. Those eyes, which enticed him while regarding him with irony, opened wide and then partly closed, as though first with sharpened attention, then in utter apathy. He felt an uneasy fondness for the stranger and yearned to solve the enigma of his mysteriousness. He watched the movements of his lips and the nervous trembling of his fingers. And suddenly the stranger seemed so oddly familiar to him: the lips were not the lips of someone unknown, but his own lips, and the hands — they were his own hands. He identified with the stranger and was so hypnotized by him that everything around seemed languorous and lethargic . . .

And now the evening bells rang out over Prague. A weight, darkly clanging and tragic, fell from their harmony. An unexpected numbness imbued the air. Stifling shadows hung drowsily over the rooftops. Not even the wing of a belated bird moved in this air. Everything suddenly seemed to be standing stock-still to listen to the conversing bells. Iron strokes broke through the windows of belfries and towers. The resonant sound cascaded down before dying out in the distance, flowing haltingly over the city's rooftops. Everything seemed to resound as in a memory — the pantiles of the roofs, slanting chimneys, rotten window frames, blind panes of glass, blackened gables, worn cornices. Prague — her past spoke in the bells, beneath the falling dusk . . .

He felt as though the long dead were speaking through the

bells. At that instant it seemed to him the immense multitude of the invisible dead was coming back to life and filling the city streets and entering the houses beneath their roofs.

Everything spoke to him of countless people who had lived here before him and yearned just as he did to finally depart into nothingness. Their hands, too, had shaken with feverish anxiety. Their pulse beat faster when they had approached the mystery. They had wanted to love, and they hurt others. They had wanted to be loved, and they felt cold. Their soul had opened deep and wide until it had recognized its own insignificance.

He was the heir of the dead. And everyone who lived here was an heir of the past. They had the eyes, the voices, the hands of the long dead. They had their desires, their passions. The history of this whole land was nothing more than the continuous revival of the same generation devoted to a mysterious work, surrendering itself to it without anyone having the fortune to see the whole . . .

The bells continued to ring.

They spoke of the bygone glory of this land, of its quarreling princes and enemies attacking the city walls. They spoke of the contemptuous townspeople and the profligate clergy, of enfeebled kings and treacherous vassals.

The sky turned red in an inundation of blood. A great phantasmagoria of burning churches and battered cloisters rose before his eyes. A gigantic black chalice was outlined against the dark red sky. Vyšehrad was falling. The walls of Hradčany were collapsing. Malá Strana was consumed in flames. The Carthusian Cloister on Újezd was veiled in the smoke of fires. And the whole earth trembled as though in an earthquake.

Prague was quiet again. The walls of churches rose. Hradčany was filled with the boisterous life of the court. And again new calamities rushed in like dark clouds weighted down with terror. The Strahov Gates saw troops fleeing the battlefield, and the Old Town Square drank the blood of the insurgents. Foreigners forced their way in throughout all the land and strangled its life.

The bells of St. Vitus were the loudest. The enormous Zikmund bell resounded with an oppressively grave, tragic knell, as though its voice desired to penetrate to the deepest spaces of the cathedral where the dead kings sleep. And the bells of Strahov and the Loreta answered, the former with a balanced melody, the latter in a mood of remote, muffled, metallic sounds drowned in the twilight and gloom. The bells of St. Nicholas sounded from below with a voice that seemed shattered in the depths of the darkness. The Maltese bells rang darkest, as though they had been lost forever among the ruins of the church tower.

And from the other side of the river the Týn bells pealed as though calling to another horrifying execution.

The Jindřich bells moaned as they once had beneath a hail of Swedish and Prussian bullets. The bells of the Franciscan Monastery recalled the abandoned church and slaughtered monks, their voices weighted with inert oppressiveness. On Charles Square the cupola rocked with the sound of bells as though remembering the distant sound of the storms that once shook it. The bells of Vyšehrad were already sinking in an immeasurable distance, as though from a long-vanished church. The bells of St. Stephen's Church grieved over the gravestones of families of long-gone lineages.

And, barely audible, it seemed the bells of vanished churches, long mute, also mingled with this chorus. Now the twilit buildings long transformed into barracks, hospitals, offices, private homes, and storehouses suddenly regained the appearance of old cathedrals and monasteries. The pedestrians in the somber, twisting, shadow-filled lanes also seemed to take on a different aspect. Their steps wavered, and they suddenly seemed clad in long, flowing cloaks, which made their figures seem longer. Their faces had grown pallid to the point of appearing stiff and dead above the folds of their starched, puckered collars, beneath their erect broad-brimmed hats.

The Middle Ages were coming to life again in the streets that narrowed in the darkness, pressing to themselves the rows of reticent houses. Night returned the city to its earlier guise and transformed the memory of bygone glory into a momentary reality . . .

He stared at the city.

His gaze drank in all those things so many others had seen before him, so many lives perished in times lost long ago. He felt their being diffused on all the walls, the dank and sweating mold. He sensed their touch clinging to all the stones, doors, and windows. He mingled his own being with the souls of the long dead, with the rhythm of their breathing. He called them forth and revived all those of whom nothing remained but nameless dust, dispersed in places where it was sometimes whipped up by windstorms to envelop the city, blown over the cobblestones, roofs, and corners of houses.

He awakened from his hypnotic state and laboriously returned to the present. He felt how foreign and vague everything was. He felt a certain harshness in all of his relations to things and alienation from the rest of the world.

Everything long past, which nevertheless stood in the background like a phantom that could not be turned away, he now sensed as the agonizing basis of the life of the present. In this city, he felt, it was entirely impossible to be free of the past.

He stood up. He was completely alone. Even the stranger had left. A dead silence had spread over the city. The sky had deepened into the darkness of cobalt. He now felt something like an intense compassion for the unknown . . .

XI

He thought for a long time about the phantasmagoria of that evening.

The Gothic still lived in Prague . . . And then again, everything was dead . . .

No, no . . . The Middle Ages still lived here . . . Something so great as religious fervor could not vanish from the world as if it had never even existed. It *had* to have left some traces . . .

But the greater the fervor once here, the greater the indifference now. Today everyone laughed at the pious delusion of the Old Czech Utraquist who saw the body and blood of God in the bread and wine and bowed low before them, and at the old Taborites and the Czech Brethren, who saw in the bread and the wine only a symbol, a residue, of the Last Supper. For this they had consigned their adversaries to Hell. All of it seemed so childish now.

Admittedly, the Czechs once competed with the entire world as great experts in matters of heterodoxy, imitating all kinds of folly, whether Arian, Manichean, Nestorian, or Waldensian, but today there was no trace of this. Nothing remained of it, nothing at all. All of this nonsense was now rotting in stuffy libraries, in thick folios, buried and forgotten, all of those exegeses, tracts, and registers, in which so much mutual Christian love had accumulated. Who would still read them before mold had completely overtaken them? That's the Middle Ages! A time of vital, ecstatic, burning faith!

But what about Chelčický?

He paused.

Of course, Chelčický was a great genius. But he had left his own time behind and transcended it so far into the future that even today he was still not fully appreciated.

Chelčický and the fifteenth century — an anachronism. What does Chelčický really have in common with Brother Gregory or Lucas van Prague, who were typical for that time? He argued with both the Utraquists and the Taborites, and in the end he certainly condemned the Brethren as well for all of their rigidity and narrow-mindedness. He condemned all "power by the sword," all spilling of blood both in war and in executions — and moreover, his ideas would still be relevant today, hardly anachronistic. Yet he also condemned all authority of man over man: offices, town councilors, district administrators, and kings. He denied judicial legitimacy and disdained the court oath.

He was a great and absolute nihilist. He was a typical Czech, because we all work toward nihilism. Nobody knows how to contest everything so grandly as a Czech, and Chelčický was so perfect at it. He would sit in his cottage and cross off one thing after another. There should be nothing in the world. Nothing at all. The tavern keeper selling beer, the merchant conducting business, the judge sitting in judgment, the mercenary fighting — all of them bring evil to the world. They should do nothing, because every activity was profane vanity and diabolical pride, and to do nothing was the foundation of all wisdom.

That was spoken to us from the soul. And this was why Chelčický was the greatest Czech philosopher. If Chelčický's philosophy were transferred from the moral and religious realm to the national and ethnic, which had not been such pressing issues in his time, it would illuminate the Czech soul that everyone has found so difficult to define. Among our mottos we have his beautiful maxim: Do nothing and contest everything.

He was getting agitated. He shouldn't be so lyrical. The poetry of errant sects appealed to him, midnight gatherings in the depths of the woods, where books were stowed in hideouts and buried in pits, then read by the light of torches amidst weeping and sighing.

This stupefied him, and everything intoxicated him with a vague romanticism. He thought himself an exceptional, medieval soul, since he was so ecstatically enamored of mold and putrefaction. He sensed a connection between his being and the medieval, and this was surely why he would become so incensed whenever someone railed against it. He had deluded himself into believing all of that. Those things were dead, and if anything remained, it was only superficial. Today's churches were nothing but services and priests. There were no believers. And those who did attend went either out of habit or for the spectacle — the bells, the kneeling, the singing, the burning incense. But their hearts and thoughts were indifferent.

Did no one believe in God anymore? he cried out.

Did he really believe in Him?

When he thought about his upbringing, how from childhood they had forced into his head the existence of some higher being that nobody had seen and in which everyone wanted to believe nonetheless, when he thought of the poetic qualities of that image (it's so seductive to imagine something higher and more perfect than ourselves) . . . he asked in the silence, in the complete silence of his soul: do I believe in God?

He froze.

In truth, I do not believe in God! echoed in his inner self. No, I have never believed in Him with full certainty! Never! Not as a child, and not now! I may have feared something mysterious and terrible that could strike me down if I didn't believe, but fear is not belief in God's existence. I called upon God in my prayers mechanically, and while I recited them I was always aware that prayers were in fact futile, that I was praying only to suppress my anxiety from the fact that I didn't believe . . . that I was praying for myself and not out of a faith in God . . .

XII

His soul was overflowing. It was not possible that those feelings had died. True, the times were marked by religious indifference. And the most profound apathy might be found in Bohemia. But this was only natural.

Czech thought was once extravagantly single-minded. Czechs ruminated and brooded too much, and thus the present stagnation was necessary for the soul to gather strength for further missions. But the religiosity of the Czech soul had not lost its vital relevance. Far from dead, it was only slumbering, a fleeting bubble breaking out above the surface. It was enough.

He recalled those he deeply respected: a poet whose mysticism invoked phantoms from the silent shadows draping his solitude; a painter from somewhere in the south, from the region that had given birth to Chelčický, and who horrified blasé thinking with the convulsive countenance of Christ, which everyone called absurd.

Souls still lived beyond the indifference of everyone who had made the boundless suffering of Christ forever grievous. The flames of ecstatic love had never been extinguished. The strength of hearts loving God had not been entirely suppressed.

Only how could he have doubted it? Was he to think, if only for a moment, that nothing more than mere words and lifeless formulae remained from that entire epoch with its atmosphere of fervent love and unshakable devotion?

There were silent and penitent souls linked to the long-gone souls who pored over the Bible in the solitude of their cottages. And what of him — was he not that kind of soul? Did he not wander the melancholy earth with a single thought — to get closer to God and find a resolution for his doubts in the peace of a believing and loving soul?

He was really raving now.

Of course, he was too frequently beset with doubt. Yet this was nothing more than his striving to find confirmed truth. In times of the most profound religious ecstasy were there not people who went up to receive the Eucharist with laughter, not even having made confession beforehand? They would spend the whole night drinking wine with womanizers, and in the morning each would take the Lord's body and blood into his hand, profaning its sanctity. He had never dared to challenge God in that way. His doubt rested only in the question: God, where are You? His doubt concerned only secondary things, only the external. And he always bowed his head to God in the end.

Mere words, words, words, he cried out, his soul suddenly despairing. After all, I don't believe in God! At least at this moment I don't believe in Him. And that's decisive. For even if I used to believe in Him, now everything is in question.

I feel that I will never actually believe in God again. It is not even possible for me to believe in Him.

I was raised not to believe in God, since from the very beginning they presented Him to me in such an absurd form that I could not help but doubt His existence. They told me such naive legends about Him that He was made laughable.

Even more — they deliberately concealed Him from me. They gave me a mere surrogate in place of Him. Where is there a church that contains God? Everywhere only Christ, Mary, and the saints — but never Him, the Only God. They taught me to kneel, recite prayers, cross myself, beat my breast, and bow my head. But they did not teach me to believe. They made me learn to hate. I was repulsed by what should have been the most holy.

I want God, not His pageantry. Imagine — I did not believe in God, and nonetheless I wanted to become His priest. What hypocrisy! How morally low I fell! How was that possible?!

He was now amazed.

I tried to mend my ways, simulating ethical ideals. How false! Ethical ideals, and faithlessness! Or did I think I would ultimately find those ethical ideals in God?

No, no, all was in vain. Despair that it was no longer possible to live in his childhood faith, which earlier had taken the place of a true faith! It was a faith in sculptures and marionettes that served as symbols of something that exists, though he could not yet understand it!

No, he knew now that he understood everything, and that what existed was nothing. He was now a staunch atheist. He had never had as much courage to realize it so precisely and clearly as now . . .

Those were mad dreams. Now in the dead silence of the night he realized everything. That's the way it was, and not otherwise. And tomorrow it might again be different. He allowed himself to think that he might again love what was dead and bow before God, in whom it was impossible to believe. But the truth would remain: it was impossible to believe in Him, even if he were to beat his forehead against the ground in penance until the end of his days.

Suddenly a church rose up out of the darkness before him. He didn't even know where he was. And he couldn't tell what church it was, yet it seemed to be saying to him: look, you who do not believe, look at me! I am here, although you deny me.

Yes, you are, he said to the church, but where are the faithful to fill your empty space with prayer?

I don't know where they have gone, replied the church. Some have died. Some have just wandered off. They will come when the world has wounded them. Despair will bring them to my steps. And they will again call upon God here, beat their breasts in penitence, and shed tears before the holy images . . .

Illusions, illusions, he interrupted. You are a tomb, not a church. Faith is dead. No one believes anymore, no one bows his head. You are so cold. There is no life in you. You are all marble and dead metal. You have transformed everything into dead matter. You have denied life. You have preached mortification and asceticism. You have terrified the world with the gaunt faces of martyrs, instead of delighting it with a smile and cheerful faith. How chilling are your crucifixes, chalices, and reliquaries! The roses of your altar drip blood from their leaves. Your altar cloths have the pallor of a corpse's vesture. Your chapels resemble jail cells. And what darkness in your depths!

I am not dead, answered the church. I am waiting patiently. The world will return. It *must* return. God wishes it.

God? he laughed. Is there really still a God? Open your tabernacles! Where do you have God? Look, the hiding place is empty! You see that only now! Where is your God? Tell me, where is your God?

But the church was silent. Now it, too, no longer existed. It had merely been a vision. The phantom of a thing long dead. A black shadow immersed in darkness. Its outlines seemed distant and utterly misshapen.

He was so distressed he could barely catch his breath. An immense weight oppressed his soul — reproach and anguish, both at once. He groaned in pain . . .

And suddenly emptiness settled in his soul . . . The vast emptiness of a space where one wants to cry out, no matter how futile it may be. No one was there to hear him. He felt that he himself was now the dead church from which God had departed, never to return.

Everything around seemed to have become frozen in silence. He thought there was not a single living being left in the world to wail to burst the oppression of that terrific silence. And he now doubted whether he was even alive himself. He moved instinctively, as though to convince himself that he was not dead . . .

Yet the silence was more eloquent than the most passionate words, which often passed him by without making the slightest impression. He felt the silence settling on his torpor like a tombstone on the dead past.

He turned and walked away. But he seemed to hear a voice in his soul: you will never efface this moment from your memory . . .

XIII

He wandered around and lay in bed for entire days. His senses seemed to have become incapable of seeing anything, hearing anything, judging, feeling interest in anything. That his dream could be revived in shades of color struck him as impossible. He knew now that there would be only nothingness.

Then came grief. Silent, patient grief. For everything. For the vanity of life, desires, all endeavors. Nothing would be possible except to conceal himself in his own being and be silent forever.

And although he felt that the death of his dream originated in his own inner self, there nevertheless came times when he blamed his surroundings, people, and the world for killing his dream.

How indifferent to his torments was everyone who crossed his path! Although he avoided people, he loved them nonetheless. He loved them from afar. He gave them appearances more beautiful than they had and feelings more beautiful than he could perceive in them.

He intended to start a new life, one purged of all sentimentality over not having found an answer.

All of these things teemed in his mind. They all occupied his thoughts.

Yet now these thoughts seemed not to emanate from his inner self, as they had before. His brain dictated them, but he could no longer think about them intimately, only direct them with logic rather than with his heart. He was now talking aloud much too often, and he sought to divert himself by observing his surroundings with a forced superciliousness.

He sensed something unexplained behind all of life. Or was he wrong? Was life lived more simply than he imagined?

His conception of life, how it should be lived in actuality, weighed on his mind. Hour after hour, day after day, from dawn to twilight. Some daily cares, conversation, smiling, pain, and that was it. And all the while the constant feeling that he was not living his life as he should, that it was only something temporary. An illusion. This was the only feeling that had any permanence in the ephemerality of everything.

Life was so dark, precarious — probably because he continually thought about it. Why wasn't he like other people? They don't think: in the morning they get out of bed, go to work, eat and drink, have fun, grieve and get angry, love and hate, so as to begin the next day all over again. And they do not lose their appetite for things repeated a hundred times over. That they already know today what tomorrow will bring does not upset them in the least. The word *why* does not exist for them; they know that everything ends with the grave, a layer of earth tossed on their dead body, nothing but a *necessity* that need not spoil the present moment.

Only he was in the habit of questioning, although he knew he would find no answer. He sought to penetrate the mystery of life, although he had no way to light its depths.

He lived so little. He did not know what living was. Everything passed without his affecting it — he was *subject* to life. His life — water flowing through a riverbed on whose direction he had no influence.

He lived only to look into his inner self. In the distance, in the colorful hum, there was a world he didn't know. He did not live with the others. He did not feel with them. He did not think with them. He was living a lie.

Yes, he was deceiving himself. Though dissatisfied, he did

not know how to approach what was foreign to him. He invented new words to calm himself, and he allowed day after day to pass him by. He did not emerge from his solitude.

He was not capable of living. He was not born for life, as a blind man is not born to see. He tried in vain to enter life, yet was destined to stand outside of it.

He was filled with an amorphous sorrow, oppressed by the awareness of being in the aimlessness of everything.

Everything seemed to be dissolving into shadows. He looked at the walls of the room that confined him in solitude, and to the dim, steely sky, through which dark clouds laboriously dragged along like apathetic images through stagnant thoughts — he perceived the paint of the walls, the windowpanes, the window frames, the roof, the sky, but in his soul only a layer of gray permeated everything. He did not understand where he was going and why he was even moving. He came to a halt, amazed to realize that he felt an aversion to walking toward any kind of destination.

Everything around him seemed to have been extinguished. All he had experienced was nothing more than a remote land he had floated past, from which nothing remained in his soul but a few disconnected fragments: stains of trees reflected on the fading sky, a man walking in the distance, a boat sailing... He recalled the words he had spoken today. He recalled the appearance of the man with whom he had conversed. It seemed he could see his lips quite distinctly. Then he remembered his mother. He saw her dead in the misty, pale yellow weeping of delicate candles dripping rivulets of hot wax. He saw her, observed her immobile hand. Would it move?

He remembered: this was the *only* impression that took hold of him when he looked at the corpse of his mother.

Everything merged together. It was all so remote — his mother's death, his youth, and his present as well. It all retreated into the unseen distance. His last intimate words (when did he speak them?), the distant ringing of the bells, the tomb . . . then gray days, transient agitation . . . everything was floating away. He was alone. As though he were cut off from everything forever . . .

XIV

After a long time he wandered up to the Barnabite Cloister again . . .

Everything was the same as ever there. The trees near the lane were rustling, but the cloister windows were lifeless.

He gazed into their stillness with such despair at the vanity of it all. Everything was so unimaginably futile that his throat constricted in anguish . . .

The Middle Ages once again surrounded him. Ascetic saints raised their emaciated arms to him. Their faces, starved by fasting, seemed to stare at him sternly.

He felt like a traitor to his own past. He fled the atmosphere of the cloister.

But the Loreta drew him like a violent power. He had to enter it.

He bowed his head before the altar inside. And he cringed like the most wretched sinner. He clasped his hands in mute prayer. A moan of despair forced its way from his throat.

But he could not pray. How could he know if God would accept his prayer? He was guilty of so much, it was not even possible for God to forgive him . . .

Forgive me, God, forgive me, he whispered mechanically. He did not even know what his lips were saying.

Deeper and deeper shadows enveloped his soul. He was there alone. No one was there to tell him: you are forgiven.

His soul was fevered and agitated.

And suddenly his gaze fell on a strange image.

At first he could not tell what it represented. The cadaverous face of a woman, sunken from fasting, shone from a flood of red hair as she bent over a skull.

The image enticed him. He had to approach, to have a closer look.

Yet the more he gazed at the picture, the more mysterious it seemed.

Suddenly the eyes appeared to gleam with something sensuous. No, that was an illusion . . . Yet those eyes full of mystery . . .

Pleasure, laughter, dance, the purple fire of perverse, rapidly withering flowers, rousing nakedness with a fragrance like caraway . . . an atmosphere of thrilling vice.

Magdalene . . .

She had walked forward through all sin. She had experienced everything, had wrung from life all its pleasures. Repulsion and exhaustion followed. Then He appeared, whom she could love, whose feet she could bathe in fragrances and wipe down with her hair. First she had to love the entire world before she could love God.

Yes, it is necessary to love the world, to taste its pleasures. Only then does one arrive at God and virtue. One must first sin, and only afterward may one become a saint. One must love to the point of madness to make renunciation possible. For how is it possible to renounce what one has not experienced and come to know?

What an illusion for the Church to give everyone a model for life and say: you shall live in accordance with this model and none other if you wish to be saved.

He wanted to burn with passion, to feel torture and pain. But the Church had taught him: be sober, impervious. Be very careful not to taint your soul, and keep your eyes shut to avoid all temptation.

That was ice, not the flame he pined for. This was not Saint Teresa in ecstasy, evoking Christ's nakedness in a convulsion. It was aloofness, icy indifference.

Again he looked into the mysterious eyes of the image. The fire of her face had gone out in icy roses, her lips trembled with laughter for the last time, and the ornaments of precious stones dropped from her breast. The quivering snow of her body was lost to death, and horror had forced the figure into a pose of despair. Yet the reflection of sensuality remained in the diamonds of her eyes, as though it still wished to intimate even now, when worldly pleasures had perished, that it was necessary to live and above all *to live* . . .

To live — to live — he repeated these words several times. Everything now lay in those words. To live life with passionate longing, open to everything it might offer. To experience everything, and find delight and sorrow equally in everything.

Meaning and beauty existed in equal measure in everything, in joy and in pain.

The air outside was oppressive. Everything was growing mute in a white glow.

Yet the ancient cloisters were imbued with something like an intense breath of life . . . It now looked more like a family gallery than a church. The saints resembled proud noblewomen, their powdered faces raised above stiff Spanish collars, framed by hair that was artificially styled and coquettishly braided with pearls. Their virtue, apparently so suspiciously cold, seemed to challenge the viewer to tempt it.

Sebastian, so slender in his exuberant nakedness, also looked too worldly, and his limbs, pierced by arrows, seemed not even to suffer heavenly pain. And Magdalene seemed to exude the scent of an entirely earthly passion.

To sin . . . that is the meaning of life, he repeated. And here, where everything spoke of death, life now triumphantly had its say.

How strangely he now prayed to life. Sensuality! Sacred sensuality, I want to give you the melancholy name of pleasure, so that you will shine with silent glory like a magic gem!

Life must be *experienced*. He recalled the seclusion of the Barnabites. What a mistake it was to renounce experience. To lock oneself away from life. What value did virtue have if it had not been tempted? *Patrona lascivorum,* granting ephemeral love in order to achieve eternal love, could disavow life, because it had known it. But those who come to the altar untouched by any man to sing monotonous psalms — did they have the right to judge life, which they did not know, and its pleasures, which they had not tasted?

Yes, one must live. He would live. How beautiful it was to be in touch with the world, to replace miserable, gray moments of existence with the fleeting and intermittent impressions that fell into his soul and bore it away in a play of light and shadows.

He would leave his gloom behind, he would stupefy himself with the rhythms of everyday life, the conversations of the multitude, to return home with the penetrating magic in his eyes of a day pleasurably spent . . .

This would mean: to be *young*. But the way he was living now: what insensible deadness!

He was present only as a body. His soul had wandered into the indistinct distance. As he dreamed, his gaze fixed on the wall, where the thoughts passing through his head left no trace. He immersed himself in unrealizable visions, apathetic toward everything that surrounded him, losing the fixity of his gaze in the throbbing waves of dreams and, even when he had emerged from them, giving the impression of someone half asleep.

From that moment he would *live*. He would go out among people, make contact with them, feel with them. He would look for a soul to whom he could surrender himself. Yes, he would put an end to his solitude. He felt relieved by that thought. He returned home almost joyful.

XV

The revitalization of that one evening had already faded by the next day.

He felt the impossibility of everything he had dreamed.

Then he started to suffer nervous attacks. He couldn't even go out due to the intense pain in his head and eyes. He drew the curtains on the windows. He lay in bed and paced the murky rooms for entire days.

He tormented his soul, leaving himself prey to his own phantoms. On his endless walks through the family chambers he would stop in front of the portrait of his young relative who had killed himself in madness. Did this same destiny await him? Madness? No . . . He must not succumb . . . That could be prevented. One must only have the *will.* And he had the will.

Despite all of the terrible pain he was suffering, if he *wanted,* he could sit at a desk now and occupy himself with something. He could master himself through *willpower,* and even go out into the streets and mingle with people and play his role among them. If only there were not such a terrible void in his soul! A void that seemed to have no end. It was deeper and broader than he could tolerate. From morning to night. Such a void. No beginning, no end. And no longing that would make him cry, nor pain that would fill his eyes with tears and relieve his soul. Only this void — in his soul, in his heart, in his mind.

Such thoughts tightened the grip of anguish in his soul, as the movement of a prisoner tightens his fetters.

After a moment it occurred to him: my brain is decaying. I am living these moments now. Yes. He recalled: this and that . . . do I still remember this? Do I remember . . . whom? He pronounced a name. A face surfaced in his memory. Is that *the* face, the face of *the one* I absolutely wanted to think about? It isn't . . . the image of the face blurred. It vanished.

Where in fact was he? In a chamber . . . Did he know in *which* chamber? The corner chamber? Or the one giving directly onto the staircase? Was he in the blue room? Yes, he knew where he was. He was in his father's study . . . Here . . . yes, here again . . .

He no longer knew exactly what he wanted to remember. I will go mad if I torment my soul *in this way*. I shouldn't tempt it *like this* . . .

He now realized that he was kneeling before the crucifix. He jumped up. He blushed in shame. What a comedy! No, what had come over him? Surely he wasn't still praying, expecting help? From someone he didn't believe in? His terrible headache was the cause. It sometimes made him unaware of what he was doing.

And what . . . if . . . at *such* a moment, when he was not in control of himself, he opened the window, completely mechanically . . . If he swung himself up on the ledge . . . then jumped . . . onto the pavement below . . . Would this be possible? Suicide — so unexpectedly.

No — no! He had to watch over himself somehow. He mustn't be so alone here. Left to the mercy of his own self. Or — even better — to flee. Outside, into the street. So many people were on the streets today. You couldn't do anything without someone stepping in to prevent it.

Yet it was possible — to be walking along the railing of the bridge, then suddenly to swing over it and hurl yourself into the water. A splash, and then you disappear into the depths. People would come running. They would look for a boat. But in the meantime you would already be dead . . .

He called for a servant. He ordered that he sit across from him and remain there with him.

The servant was so horrified by his master's feverish eyes that he wanted to send for a doctor. No — he didn't want a doctor, and moreover, the servant should make his bed and prepare a cold compress for his head. He would be fine by morning. He just needed to lie down.

After a short time he told the servant go. He was repelled by the impeccable way the servant held his body as he attended to him.

He couldn't stand it in bed. He jumped out and knocked a chair onto his foot. The physical pain brought him somewhat to his senses.

Why was he making such a fuss today? As if he had lost his mind. What a comedy! To walk around with such thoughts! He noticed the pain had somewhat subsided. Yes, now he felt better. Only his head hurt a little . . . almost nothing. He would go out . . .

He started to dress.

He would forget in the streets. The noise would distract him a bit. It would shred the tangled tissue of his sickly dreams.

He yearned to speak with someone alive, rather than merely crying out into emptiness. He yearned to speak the ancient words about old longings and dreams. Old truths, even if they were now nothing but illusions.

He wanted to speak intimately with anyone at all. To forget trivial disputes and to love. Everyone. To love everything about them. Simply not to want to *scrutinize* everything!

It was an enemy of man who invented the maxim: "Know

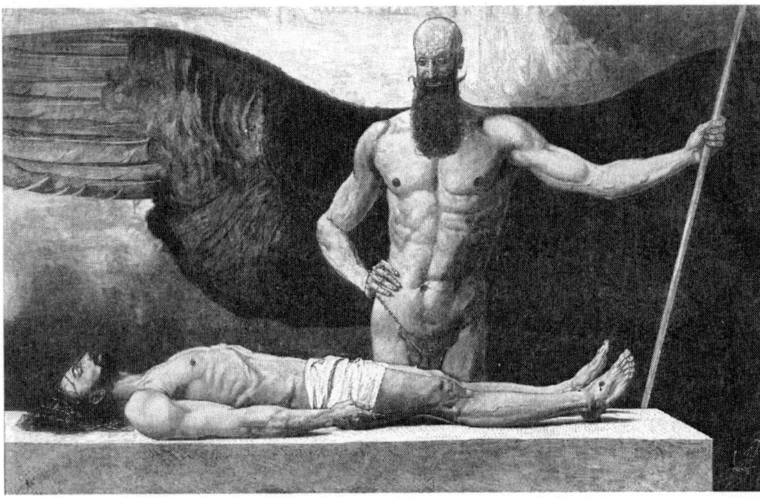

thyself." That is the same as saying: "Despise thyself." For it makes a difference whether we love or despise. And it is better to love our limited nature than to say to ourselves in the name of wisdom: you are nothing, disgusting, worthy of being despised . . .

Twilight was falling outside. Things were losing their color in the growing flood of gray.

He undressed again without going out. A sullen evening saturated with cold came scowling through the window. The faded gray of the naked sky spread across the city, and the sun was setting, lusterless as a plaque covered in ash.

This is all that remains of my life — standing at the window, he looked out stiffly, with a silent, involuntary groan the thought had put on his lips. His eyes roamed over the large area of the city that appeared before his gaze.

It was a petrified sea of rooftops, blackened pantiles, roofing tiles and bricks, distinguishable in the foreground, indistinct in the distance, and merged into a single filthy hue at the farthest point. Dead waves foamed up from the sea, rearing up forcefully, then seemingly crushed. Now solid parallel lines appeared as the crests of waves in apparent confusion, running to the horizon in every direction; now the gaze lost the lines of the compressed rooftops in the dispersion of the whole.

It was like a terrified stampede of a confused mob, the panic of a fearful multitude before the specter of a rapidly diffused horror — but a stampede without movement or screams, mute, which gave only the impression of distress.

And it kept rising, as though enormous multitudes were pushing one another on a stairway situated in a vast space. The further away, the denser the mob, until on the horizon line everything merged into a single slate-gray band, above which hung the turbid remoteness of the sky, pierced by the spikes of towers, gloomy and suffused with smoke.

A feeling of hopelessness took possession of him, anxiety from a life harried amidst the press of the crowd.

What was he looking for down there from those indifferent people? All was vanity. Hopelessness cast him into the old despair, as a hearth whose fire has gone out returns to darkness.

He felt that illness was creeping into his body. He had been able to stop it only momentarily by an overexertion of his will. A fateful period of his life was approaching. He sensed it.

The end was not yet near. He had to fight. And he would fight. To the very last . . .

Should he consult a doctor? That would be futile. What could a doctor diagnose, when the sickness was *within?* And in any case, he had always abhorred the overbearing contempt of doctors, who displayed such self-assurance because all one's hopes were placed in them, as if good health or death were solely in their power — a humiliating feeling that every sick person experiences when being treated by a doctor.

No . . . he wouldn't send for the doctor. At least *today* he wouldn't.

And he walked again from chamber to chamber. And darkness slowly grew in every corner. Then nightfall . . .

XVI

He was shivering with cold, and his teeth were chattering. He was babbling nonsense.

And suddenly something very odd happened to him.

The door opened, very quietly, and just as quietly a man entered the chamber. He closed the door noiselessly behind him, looked around, then remained standing by the nearest armchair, leaning against it.

He was a bit over thirty years old. His face was white as chalk, almost cadaverous, framed with thick hair and whiskers of that blackest hue with which dark things are reflected on the surface of water on a moonless night. They gave his face an unusually sullen and stern appearance.

Cold seemed to emanate from his high forehead. His eyes remained merciless and motionless beneath his brows, which cast no shadow on them but left them open. They looked straight ahead, without straying right or left, without the play of sidelong glances. His gaze was almost unnaturally firm.

His entire face seemed dead except for his lips, which moved barely perceptibly at times as he exhaled, and his chin, which trembled slightly.

In comparison with his face, his wide shoulders and powerful body seemed almost athletic. Beneath his long, flowing robe one could sense a strong chest and lungs and sturdy hips.

Thus stood the Stranger, not so much challenging as reproachful. It was as though he wanted to say that they would not be separated so easily. That he would carry out the intention with which he had come no matter what it took . . .

He seemed vaguely familiar. He remembered he had seen *this* man. He couldn't remember where.

He did not dare address the visitor. He waited for the Stranger to start. Yet the visitor was silent, his eyes rigid on his face.

Then suddenly he started to babble.

I know you . . . I know. I know who you are. And I knew you would come . . . this very day . . . *this very hour* you would come. I am ready. Speak. Yes, I was expecting you. I am glad that I can settle matters with you. Begin. I am waiting. Reproach me.

You do not reproach me? You stay silent? Very well. I will not get upset.

What do you want to say to me then? Do you want to blame me for doubting and denying everything in the end? You know, everything: God, people, you and me, the whole world. Yes, chastise me.

All is already dead. And it's *your* fault. Not mine. *You* have killed it, not I. You should have allowed me to be born different from what I am.

Look, now *I* am going to reproach you: for everything that has dissolved into nothingness, everything that I have left behind, for all of that I blame *you*.

The Stranger smiled wanly, though it was impossible to tell if it was a sneer or from embarrassment.

Yes, smile. Smile. I'm babbling nonsense. Obviously. But shouldn't you be ashamed, isn't what I said the truth?

We are completely alone here, and moreover, you are no longer of this world. If I weren't here, you would not be able to appear so suddenly, since in fact you do not exist, and since — you are a figment of my imagination.

Aha . . . I caught you . . . You shuddered. Be afraid of me. I'm not afraid of you. For I am your master. I will command you and you will disappear. I warn you. It's very risky to scoff at me.

I did not come to ridicule you, the Stranger said quietly, almost submissively.

Ridicule?! Do you want to fulfill my destiny? Do you really still have me in your power? Did I not renounce obedience to you? Didn't I tell you that *you do not exist?* At least for me you don't exist? My destiny is in my hands. It will be *my* hand that decides my fate . . . Not yours . . .

He started to cross the room, turning away from the Stranger. At once he seemed to remember something, halted near the Stranger and looked him in the eye.

Go somewhere else, Stranger, he said, his tone altered. There is nothing more for you here to destroy, if you've come with evil intent. And if your intentions are good, there is nothing here for you to protect.

These wounds will never heal. Never. And I don't need *new ones*. The old wounds will kill me quite reliably. For what purpose then would we desire the honor of paying each other a visit? Unless it were to torment one another. Surely you are not that malicious . . . For it must not be very pleasant even for you, I believe, to see me like this. Isn't that so?

An awkward moment passed. The Stranger did not reply. Silence descended from his lips with a cruelty that was more horrifying than the executioner's footsteps on the stairs to the condemned.

He felt as though he were looking into an unknown abyss. He was amazed that he did not collapse before that gaze . . .

I know who you are, he now said to him quietly. You are the one who taught weakness, instead of making humanity strong. You taught people not to be cheerful and happy, and commanded they be gloomy and unhappy. Strength, health, greatness — all of that you taught us to deny. You said to us: blessed are the weak, the sick, the humble . . . You hated life and brought death to the world. And you want us to be grateful for that?

Yes, we don't believe you anymore, because we want to be cured of illness. Enough with sickness, castration, and loathing. You have tormented our minds, our hearts. We do not yearn for your heaven — to arrive there tormented from our miserable earthly life. Do not think that I'm saying this because I'm suffering from a nervous disorder. No, it is precisely such disorders that lead to you, not away from you.

My soul, my being is speaking to you. A soul and a being that yearn for health and vigor. Yes . . . that is all I wanted to say to you. Why do you not protest? Speak! Deny it! Persuade me! If you can . . . Ah, that's the thing: you cannot . . .

He moaned sickly:

Don't torment me! Leave! Why are you torturing me? Why are you standing there, if you don't want to answer me?

Do you just want to reproach me? Go! Go, Silent One! That is your only strength: silence! You want to vanquish me with patience, as I am impatient! Yes, that's what you want; but look, I am not afraid! Run away now! You are in my power! So — now I have closed the door. Where will you go *now?* Where? Speak!

The Stranger retreated to the back of the room.

He approached him. Now he was just three, now two steps away.

The Stranger suddenly raised his hands. The mystical stigmata shone on them.

He cried out, awestruck. Yes, it was Him.

He dropped to his knees. He stretched out his arms and embraced the Stranger's legs.

Then he awoke. He was kneeling before the crucifix, embracing the legs of the Crucified One.

Someone was knocking at the door. It was the servant, who had come with a light and had been knocking for some time.

Go for the doctor in the morning, he ordered the servant. Or better, go for him now. It seems I am coming down with a fever.

And he suddenly collapsed, unconscious.

XVII

A lengthy illness overtook him.

At first he was unconscious. When he regained consciousness, he saw a nun at his side. Her facial features were delicate and at the same time sickly. The nun smiled kindly and gave him medicine.

He could not explain the connection between her appearance and the fact that he was bedridden.

How did she come to be here? Why was her face so grave despite her kindliness? What did the assortment of phials mean? And the washbasin? The compresses?

These were foolish questions. He was sick. But he wanted so much to ask.

At the same time he felt an especially blissful feeling quivering inside: satisfaction that they were taking such good care of him. And a touching joy that he had overcome the illness and there was still hope for health . . .

He nearly felt like crying. He felt compelled to say something especially kind, immediately, at this very moment, to his nurse. A feeling of gratitude permeated his soul. And his being blazed up. He wanted to live. He didn't want to die. He had to live.

The nurse was talking to him. The sound of her voice confused him even more, for the weight of pain spoke from its meek accent.

Such a great silence entered into his soul. Everything from the past was settled.

When he got up and the doctor first gave him permission to go out for a drive again, he felt especially cheerful.

He felt a new life was beginning. For magic and beauty lay only in the anticipation of future days.

And he knew that the happiness of his next life would lie only in its simplicity and peace. In the concentration of the two. Glorious white lines. The blue of the heavens. The sun. Noontime silence. Transparent distances. Gratitude and love for everything that is called the world.

He trembled with life like foliage in the sun.

His soul was broadening. All surfaces seemed to be renewed. Colors were more intense. Desire was more than desire.

Sounds were purer. People's faces were more beautiful. And

everything seemed to have new meaning: the gables of the houses, the entranceways, the sidewalks, the carriages, and with it all the noise of the animated street . . . the power of impressions, the flexibility of bodies, the trembling feverish activity . . . and the bridge over the river was especially beautiful, and the voices of people . . . and the reflections of light . . . Everything was so confusedly alive . . . And at the same time so intimate and simple . . .

He was driving past a church. He ordered the driver to stop, and he went in.

It was dead and cold there. Outside there was such commotion and the warmth of the young sun.

He fell to his knees. He clasped his hands and wanted to pray. Yet all this he did mechanically. He did not know why exactly he had come here, why he was kneeling here, why he wanted to pray here.

The words of the prayer did not come either — only the thought to ask for forgiveness. But from whom and why — that he no longer knew.

He now expected a singular sensation to enter suddenly into his soul. Nothing happened.

He could never forget that moment. He left disappointed and got into the carriage. His nonexistence had been decided. He felt it.

He ordered the driver to take him home.

He rode through the same streets. Sorrow and shadows now lay upon everything. The houses were gloomy, people's faces wrinkled and ill-humored, and despite the warmth of the sun, he was cold.

All of the tumult of the streets was foreign to him. The voices of pedestrians, the rattle of carriages, the clatter of hoofs on the pavement, and the letters on signboards, blurred by rain.

He then happened upon a funeral procession right on the bridge. He watched the retinue in hopeless depression, as though they were carrying his own corpse past him.

When his carriage started up again, it wasn't going fast enough for him. He asked the driver to speed up. But he was uneasy nonetheless.

Despite all the movement he felt immobile. He clenched his fists nervously.

Hopelessness overpowered his soul. Now he knew that he had not recovered from his illness. It had retreated only for a moment. It would soon return and attack him with a renewed vigor even more violent than before . . .

He still retained some hope. He grasped at it desperately, and even though he knew that *hope was an illusion,* he held onto it with all his strength.

He might still be able to *overcome* the illness. And even if it proved impossible, *normally* impossible, an *exception* could not be ruled out. It may not please others if in *this* particular case he were to triumph over his distraught organism, but he alone could and *must* overcome this illness, precisely because it was *him* and *not someone else* . . .

At times he would ask himself why he lived this senseless, unnatural life. He pondered and asked:

What does it mean to live? Is it suffering? Experiencing?

He did not know.

He remained frozen in place, reflecting.

I don't live well, he said at last. I have never lived well. From my earliest childhood, in my childhood dreams, in fairy tales ... Perhaps ... But then ... and now ...

He saw stains where he had previously seen light.

I have never known what it means to live. I have considered my vices to be virtues, my laziness to be work, myself to be a paragon and everything else a caricature.

What now? What now? The thoughts seemed to cut into his brain. Continue to live miserably? Or really live? And *how* should I live?

He hearkened to his inner voice, but the voice no longer answered him.

It's too late, he thought. It's too late! I'm lost.

He trembled.

I cannot regain my senses, I cannot remedy a thing, I have destroyed everything. If all is not yet lost, it certainly will be very soon, for I do not know *how to live*.

He felt crushed by the weight of this sudden realization.

XVIII

The doctor advised him to take a trip.

He welcomed the idea. A change of surroundings would bring him relief. Above all, he would be free from memories of the past. Maybe a torrent of new impressions would be able to whip the illness out of him.

Illusion animated his hope, as a breeze animates dry leaves on graves.

He took the train, not knowing where. He wanted to go

somewhere around the Salzburg lakes, though he hadn't made a definite decision.

As the train was leaving Prague, he was distressed at first, but his melancholy soon passed. He stared into the darkness and listened to the train roaring through the nighttime landscape. Peace infused his soul, as if from the deathly silence of the uninhabited black emptiness outside.

He rode like that, alone, for a long time. Finally his attention to the immediate surroundings flagged.

Other things, now remote, emerged in his memory. Streets, churches, palaces . . . And a bridge . . . Beneath it a deep, dark pool, and still water. Reflections of the moon in the water, trembling rays of light, like spilt silver and mercury, as though someone were using the moon as a reflector. All was enveloped in sadness, as though something great and glorious had died . . . Phantasmagoria . . . He cowered before it all. Image after image passed . . . He no longer had either strength or willpower.

Someone entered the compartment. He was roused from his thoughts. He looked around, distracted.

Where was he again? What did he want there? Who was this man who had just entered?

The newcomer was racked by a fit of coughing.

He looked him over with great wonder.

He perceived profound suffering in his face. He was quite young.

His comeliness caught his attention. He was so pale, delicate, gentle in a feminine way. And he had beautiful lips. His illness had imbued them with such a deep red.

His eyes were like two unsolvable mysteries, and they

seemed absorbed in strange fates. His cheeks had the tinge of roses starting to wither. And his hands . . . they possessed the same intelligence as his face, the same expressiveness, the grace of sickly pallor, as though they were chiseled from dull ivory.

The stranger returned his gaze with a bow of his head, which disoriented him even more.

The train was stopping. They were at a rather large station. He heard strange voices from outside, and the clash of the train cars as they were shunted to the adjacent tracks.

He looked out. People with lanterns were passing outside. Here a face shone, suddenly illuminated; there, a bit of the track as a lantern was lowered. Elsewhere he saw a hand carrying a lantern.

Again the train began to move. Again the monotony of the ride, the roar of the train. Again memories, so reproachful now. Again the man sitting across from him, silent, so young and hopelessly lost to death . . . Again his lips, so intensely red like the flowers of bloody sage, and his hands, as pale as an old man's . . .

He felt pain from his presence, and a languorous charm from his demeanor and conduct, in which there was something Anglicized, impeccable.

His gray clothing, that silver hue that so stupefies the senses, made it seem that lassitude had passed into the stranger's entire figure, into his gaze and movements. Everything about him was languid.

They did not speak a word to one another. The young man got off at one of the stations, where a lackey was already waiting for him.

He watched as he walked away. Then melancholy took possession of him again.

He remembered the name of the station where the stranger had gotten off, and on a map he looked for the names of all of the estates in the immediate surroundings and tried to guess from what family he may have come.

He ultimately settled on the name of a count's family that sounded proud and glorious, whose last bearer he imagined to be the young man wracked by illness. He desired a more intimate relationship with him, and it pained him that he had failed to introduce himself.

It pained him most of all that they would probably never meet again. He would never see the places where he lived, and he would never hear anything about him. He would never even know his true name.

He cut his trip short.

His head was starting to hurt.

After he had rested, he rode back to Prague. He was suddenly overwhelmed by the fear that something unusual, exceptionally terrible, would happen to him if he traveled further. With the determination typical of such rash decisions, he gave up all thought of staying anywhere other than at his family home in Prague.

As he passed the station where the stranger had disembarked the day before, he peered through the window. He wanted to see if he could glimpse any trace of a château, but he saw only a monotonous plain, a dusty highway, and an avenue lined with half-withered trees — not a sign of a nobleman's residence anywhere.

He stared out at the landscape in amazement, with the impassive perception of places now seen in daylight that were first glimpsed in darkness.

What had happened to the impression of last night? Had he met, for the first time in his life, someone who could have solved his nameless mystery? Or was the appearance of the young man from yesterday not perhaps a figment of his diseased imagination? Did he exist at all? It was possible that all this was just a dream . . .

How could he be certain that he was not fantasizing last night in the train? He trembled. Would he still be able to master his senses tomorrow and the next day, to keep madness at bay?

XIX

As the train pulled into Prague, he again resolved to begin a new life. He again appealed to his strength of will. It would be enough to give up all of his foolishness.

Most importantly, he should live like other people, without the caprices that made even his own company unbearable to him.

The noise of the train station in Prague, its workers running to and fro, the rush of arriving passengers to the exits — everything filled him with anxiety. He was so enervated, he could barely even get into the carriage, and he staggered when he put his foot on the step.

He cowered inside the carriage so as not to see anything on the streets he passed through.

He didn't want to see anything from that world, anything that bore traces of people, anything that was close to life.

He had been dead to everything for a long time and had made himself ill. For him everything had become an indistinct noise, flowing without flavor or color in a nebulous space toward a nebulous goal . . .

A deceitful phantasmagoria of life . . . just cast a reflection of light, the most flattering tinge, provide some musical accompaniment, and all of the foulness hidden just beneath the surface of life is forgotten.

People forget. So easily. They sit in lighted restaurant gardens, where there are a few wilted oleanders and blaring music, and they talk nonsense to one another, and this satisfies them. The next day they go window-shopping, or sometimes they stop by a church, cross themselves before the altar, yawn, dawdle for a while by the altar paintings, cross themselves again, bow, and then leave the church with a light and supple step. And nothing bothers or torments them, such as the thought that their relationship to God and faith is not at all clear or settled. For after all, what is religion for them? If sinning disgusts them, they pray. Stop sinning? Not at all — merely a rest before continuing to pursue pleasure.

As for him — how dislocated he was, pierced through! How wounded he was by life! Whenever he was ill from himself, from seclusion, he would throw himself into society. Yet it did nothing to quell his anxiety. When people told jokes around him, he was sad. When it was boisterous, he was so quiet.

Everyone was buoyant and garrulous, only he was unfriendly toward them, and he was even lonelier among them than at home, for their health and cheerfulness were right in front of him. In the end he became so annoyed he was tempted to yell at them, to express his scorn for them, to spit in their faces . . .

He would jump up and leave, furious that everything was so miserable and stupid. At the same time, he felt unhappy that he could not participate in anything or confide in anyone. They would all laugh at him if he were to confide his thoughts — if he told them that the possibility of faith in God left him vexed. There were many, many other things besides, which he could not even put into words. He had to try to master himself. Play his role in the comedy. Deceive in appearances, as though his inner self were like others'. How long could he keep it up?

The days that followed were almost all the same. In the morning he would get up with the thought that this was the day: *this* day and no other he would choose to be the start of his long awaited and desired *new life*. Making an effort to go out into the streets, he stopped by the nearest church, sat in a pew in a corner so that no one would notice him, looked at the paintings in frames shining with old gold, and attempted to pray.

He did this persistently day after day. He himself didn't even know the reason, but the need to *reconcile with God* was essential to his image of a *new life*. So he waited for a miracle, the return of faith to his heart.

His prayers would always begin with: God, I know how I have offended You. But I also know that You are merciful and that You will forgive me if I show contrition for the sin I have committed so basely. My God . . . My God . . .

His prayer would get stuck there.

He gazed at the altar, and it would suddenly seem ridiculous to him that he was sitting in a pew and praying such nonsense . . . To whom? To the altar. He did not believe in anything, and here he was praying . . . with such ardor, to what? To deaf things.

And the altar — how disgustingly bedecked it was. With what barbarous taste! The newly restored painting almost screamed with color. And wasn't that gilded angel — just a bit too chubby? The paper roses, the prayers framed in glass, the pillow on the prayer book, the cover stitched with tiny pearls . . . what a toy . . . the strips of tin, the gilding, the little fragments of glass . . . all in the utter naïveté of an antiquated legend . . .

He would leave the church annoyed. Ashamed of himself, he would return home. With the apathy of a man who knows he will get nowhere no matter how long he waits, he would spend the whole day walking around his room or lying in bed.

He liked to assure himself that he would sacrifice *this* day to the old way of life and tomorrow (most certainly) he would start his *new life,* while aware (most certainly) that the next day would be exactly the same as this one, that all of his efforts to forcibly put an end to his life as he had lived it were doomed to fail.

Nights tormented him most. Sleepless nights. During the day at least his surroundings provided some distraction. Night, however, would give him up entirely as prey to his hallucinations. He would be sitting — and suddenly it seemed that something was happening behind him, *something extraordinary*.

He turned around — silence everywhere. He did not see or hear anything.

He stood up and paced the room. He heard a sigh in the next chamber. He opened the door fearfully. Nothing was there.

He sat down again, and again it seemed that some shadow was rising up behind him.

He sat motionless for a while. He waited to see what would happen. Now the shadow leaned over him, now it was looking over his shoulder, and now . . .

He screamed. He jumped up. His eyes were so strange, as though they had seen even stranger things. And again nothing.

It was but an illusion. No one was there. He walked around. It went everywhere with him. It never left him alone. It persecuted him. It forced him to make gestures he could not control.

He welcomed daybreak as liberation.

Yet after a brief respite the torments would start over again. Day after day passed, and his illness worsened until it became unbearable.

XX

He noticed on the daily calendar that it was the name day of his last living aunt. She was the mother of the cousin who had died quite young in a fit of religious mania. He hadn't been to see her for several years. It suddenly occurred to him that he should pay her a visit.

She lived in one of the strangest houses in Malá Strana,

uninhabited by anyone but her for several decades now. Since her son's suicide she had given all of her tenants notice one by one and had not taken on any others. Apartment after apartment became empty and filled with dust and cobwebs, until no one but she and an old, completely deaf maidservant lived in one of the courtyard wings of the large house, which resembled a cloister.

When he approached the house and saw its desolate façade and dusty windows with broken panes yawning here and there, he was taken aback, and he wondered whether his aunt still lived there.

He opened the gate and went into the entryway. It was full of all kinds of junk — and no trace of anyone anywhere.

He went up the stairs to the second floor and was astounded to see Christ on the cross hanging opposite the staircase, enveloped in cobwebs.

The hallway was empty. He opened the door to an entrance hall. No one was there.

He continued on and stumbled over a clay pot that had been left behind by the last tenants to move out. He entered a room with a view of the street. It, too, was empty. All that remained of the people who had once lived there were lighter spots on the walls where pictures had once hung and several nails in the walls. He returned to the hallway and walked around the entire floor.

He finally stopped by an old, rusty, metal-plated door.

He tugged the bell-pull. No sound. The connection had been severed.

He knocked loudly. Still no one came.

He grasped the handle and opened the door. It was not locked. He peeked inside. No one was there. Yet the appearance of the room indicated that it was inhabited.

He opened and partially closed the door behind him. Now he was in darkness. He went up to the next door by memory. He knocked again.

No one answered. He opened the door and entered the next room. No one was there either. There was a bed with a canopy and an enormous old oak cabinet, as one finds in archives.

He continued through several rooms. One of them resembled a museum of antiques, in it about five clocks ticking with the voice of clocks of past epochs, a melancholy plaint. One was in a glass case, and another was decorated with the goddess Nike on a triumphal chariot; a standing clock resembled a wine barrel borne aloft by two dragons, with the figure of a faun on top. On the table stood a clock that looked like a small cabinet with the face on the upper level, and suddenly from somewhere in the corner a musical clock began to play. The cheap tinkling of a long forgotten melody filled the room.

It was so dark in one of the rooms that he did not immediately notice the door concealed behind the portière.

He didn't even knock before he entered the next room, so curious he was to see if he would find anyone there. In the little room, filled with all manner of trinkets and embroidery and with the musky scent of wilted flowers and dead family costumes, an old-fashioned easy chair stood in the back opposite the door, and an old woman sat in the chair with her head bent down into her lap and her feet buried in pillows spread out on the floor.

He recognized his aunt. She did not seem to notice him. Her eyes were fixed on a single spot on the ground. They looked glassy. Perhaps she was dozing. Perhaps she was thinking about something. She seemed petrified, and cadaverously yellow. He then noticed she was reading from a piece of paper.

He announced himself, speaking her name. She wasn't listening.

He took a few steps toward her. Even then she didn't notice him. He placed his hand on her shoulder. Then she goggled at him. She screamed, leaped up, and tried to take a step. She staggered and raised her arms against him. And suddenly she started to babble like a madwoman.

— Vilém — that was the only thing he understood of the incoherent sounds gushing from her throat.

He realized she thought he was her dead son. She had, it seemed, gone completely mad with grief and age.

He said his name and started to talk to her, trying to calm her down. But she had begun to weep convulsively. She finally recognized him.

Out of a small cabinet she took the old pistol Vilém had used to shoot himself, then she took out the prayer book in which she kept his last letter, ruled as if by a child, written in very large script that announced he was ending his life. It was evident from the letter that he had gone mad from the *idée fixe* that a new Judas had been born into the world who would again betray the Savior. She babbled and laughed like a child. She showed him these relics as she told him about all the various relatives who were already long dead, many of whom he had never even known, as though they were still alive.

Again she called him Vilém, and she pressed him to sit down.

He left.

Near the gate below he encountered his aunt's old servant, returning from the market. She goggled at him, laughed like a half-wit, then continued on her way without paying him any mind. She, too, was evidently mad and took care of the household entirely mechanically, following old habit.

A great misfortune, a terrible family catastrophe had impressed in these two old brains the same images forever, just as the traces of dead plant life are imprinted in fossils.

XXI

Day after day passed, empty and futile. Feebly he dragged himself through them, as a shadow passes by without leaving a trace . . .

When he remembered all he had experienced it was as if he were looking at a landscape immersed in dusk: everything oppressed with the melancholy of expiration, vanishing slowly in veils of gray — colors fading, light waning, objects receding.

But the space grew. The sky deepened and heightened ever more vertiginously — the indifferent sky, without moon and stars, the autumn sky. Then everything merged into one black pool. One more person appeared on a path, then vanished, and he, still thinking he was being pursued, now observed how mournfully the shadows merged . . .

He seemed to be peering into the dead past, and he encountered a long funeral procession, trudging along indolently through the dusky phantom landscape — a long retinue, a melancholy crowd, from which sorrow, hopelessly distressing, fell and beat on his soul as if it were the muffled and hollow drums of a funeral march. He recognized the procession, the participants, and he thought he should call them back and apologize for being so apathetic in letting them leave him, for his frequent petulance toward them, for abhorring them.

The procession was already far away. It was no more than a line, undulating obliquely in the infinite, an insubstantial stain. Then nothing could be seen at all. All that remained was the horizon, its contours, the emptiness of the plain — silence, death.

Everything was dead to him now. The present belonged to other people; it gazed at other hopes and other despairs.

Sighs escaped his constricted breast. Tears dried up in his lifeless eyes. The footprints of others spread traces of spilt blood and trampled the unbearable tension of the pain that afflicted him. He retreated forever from his joy like a pedestrian from closed gates.

He cut himself off completely from the world. He stopped going out as regularly. He did not receive anyone.

He often secluded himself entirely. He now lived in a completely different world from others. He had nonetheless maintained some contact with people of late, but only with considerable effort, and how cold and false it all was!

There was only one possibility now: seclusion.

He was alone everywhere, wherever he went. Whether at home, roaming the streets, distant from the places, the people, and the things among which he walked, or hiding somewhere

in a church. Day after day passed. He lost track of time. He only felt himself aging. And as time passed, he grew colder. The world that appeared before his eyes was no longer the world of his youth. He had expected so much from the world of his youth — from today's world he expected nothing.

Even dead things were changing. Houses were disappearing, giving way to new ones. New streets were appearing, and old ones were lost. The new lacked the intriguing, sorrowful shadows, the mystery proper to everything old. An alienating, cold emptiness wafted from everything.

Sometimes he tried to read recent books, but he couldn't finish a single one. The atmosphere in them was no longer the atmosphere of his former dreams, now dead.

There were moments when he felt, rather than peace, a kind of deadness in his soul. Nothing new came to him; nothing from the past caused him pain. And he was thankful. At least for a while, the sickly agitation, which made him aware of *himself,* would abate. He would forget, lose himself, and *cease to exist*. This was now the only thing that could bring him some relief.

Yet the most silent sorrows are the greatest of vanities.

He again had sudden fits of childishness. He would cry, hiding his face in a pillow. He yearned to be stroked and caressed. He would get up after hours of complete depression, ashamed of his sentimentality.

But sometimes he was afflicted by sentimentality even when he was out.

A strange thing happened to him one evening. He was wandering through the battered, filthy streets of the Jewish Town.

He came upon the Old-New Synagogue, dead, sunken as into the mold of tombs, where a livid ray of light falls through the narrow Gothic windows like a feeble flash of the present.

Inside, he huddled in a black corner.

A cantor was singing in drawn-out notes in the suffocating stench of the oil lamps, in the darkness, and it was like a lamentation over the dead past and a nation crushed by futility: the congregants, heads bowed, somberly lamented the destruction of Jerusalem.

It was something so dismal and despairing, he had to leave so as not to be suffocated by the sorrow. The vanity of all things oppressed him too tangibly.

Now he was even afraid of his own voice. Every sound frightened him. He had turned into an object tortured by the whole of his surroundings. Everything stabbed him.

The most horrifying images formed in his imagination. All the ugliness and sickliness of life merged into revulsion.

Agitated by the apprehension that something was unexpectedly strangling him, he would get up at night filled with horror.

He would turn on the light only to be horrified again by the shadows on the pallid walls, where something grim and cadaverous trembled as on sheets beneath a corpse . . . It was true: the shadow seemed alive. It grew and shrank, extending something grotesque like the tentacle of a nocturnal monster pulling a late-night prank. Now he was afraid of himself . . .

XXII

He started to seek out pilgrimage sites.

He recalled how he had once by chance seen a procession walking through the woods on trails full of rose heath. This had left a profound impression in his soul. The fervent, ancient song of the Holy Virgin, resounding beneath the crowns of the trees, the red of the banners waving gaily above the group, the bright white dresses of the bridesmaids carrying a small marionette replete with gold and silk — all of this had become magically fixed in his soul.

He looked for impressions such as this again. He went to Svatá Hora, Holy Mountain. He visited Stará Boleslav. Yet everything appeared so sober and banal.

He went to Dobrá Voda near Budějovice and drank from the spring of miracle-working water and prayed entirely alone in the church.

He traveled to Filipsdorf on the border with Saxony, where he had never been before. He experienced several moments of hysterical excitement there in the miraculous cottage where Mary had once cured the gravely ill. He threw himself to the ground, wept, ardently kissed the earth, and whispered incoherent prayers. God, God, have mercy! Mary, heal me! Do not judge my iniquities! Have pity on my wretchedness! I have judged myself. My God, miraculous Mary, be merciful to me when I cannot be merciful to myself! Heal me!

He sobbed like a madman.

He went once more to Filipsdorf. But the magic of the first visit was gone. The church was an utterly tasteless modern edifice. The Chapel of the Virgin Mary was disfigured by color prints dedicated to the place by those Mary had healed and by the crutches they had cast aside. There was a rather ordinary clay pot of holy water by the altar in which believers dipped rosaries and medallions. And there was a fair around the church, a gaudy amalgam of tawdry stalls . . .

As he was waiting at the station for the train from Ebersbach in Saxony, he met a young man who revived for a time his old yearnings for friendship.

The stranger greeted him and, bored in the lonely station, attempted to start a conversation. He finally gave up after meeting only with silence.

They looked at each other. He was astonished at the stranger's comeliness, a touch of feminine beauty mingled with the swarthiness of mature masculinity.

All the way back to Prague he was afflicted by a mysterious anxiety; the profound impression gave rise to remorse. The stranger's face, such expressive features and such tense expectation coupled with such openness, now reproachfully occupied his mind. Had he not been someone he should have gotten to know? Had destiny purposely arranged their encounter so as to bring resolution to his confused soul, which had betrayed itself? But he had rebuffed him, had missed the opportunity to become friends. What was the nature of the magic that opened the door for one person to connect in life with another? What was the mysterious power that led one to identify with someone else, and with such force that it was not possible for them to part, or at least not for long, a passionate friendship he had yet to know, the union of two bodies as well as the union of two souls?

The anxiety still plagued him when he arrived in Prague. It intensified in the sultry summer night hanging inertly over the city in expectation of a storm.

The lights glowed red in the burning air. The noise of passersby in the streets and singing from the beerhalls and the music of brass instruments playing in restaurant gardens — all of it seeming to vibrate in the overburdened air. It made everything sleepy and defenseless. It killed slowly yet irrevocably . . . Then an ominous red flash in the sky frightened him. He could sense the anger of imminent lightning that would flash wildly across the sky as the atmosphere thickened.

The moon beneath the dark clouds was unusually large and somber like a copper plate.

Were these not the diseased perceptions of an organism in decay? Did others see and feel all of this too? He looked around anxiously and tried to read their faces, but he did not find anything to read.

So this is the end of everything, his lips whispered. Will I continue to live? Is it even possible to live?

He had allowed his entire life to pass him by. So many people had walked past him, and he hadn't called out to a single one. Distrusting everyone, he had avoided them. He had hidden himself in seclusion, where everything disgusted him.

He had hoped, loved, hated in vain. There was nothing in any of it, not in love, not in hate. He had done no harm to anyone, nor had he done any good. He walked through space as a cipher, a shadow along a wall. His eyes deep in sleep, he thought he was awake.

Yet still he had felt there was something in him, a possibility of life, though he did not know where he should make a stand, where to begin. He felt he was neither the worst, nor the very last; it seemed to him that he had failed to fully create himself, had left himself incomplete. He had been waiting for his time to come. But it had not come, and his life had been wasted in vain . . . Only his dreams existed . . . only his dreams! . . .

It was time to quiet his soul. Everything that burned uneasily within it must be extinguished. May others live. He would watch them calmly, those he was indifferent to, watch their endeavors, which were foreign to him. As for him . . . he would live, without knowing why . . .

Why delay? It was the end. The hour had struck. He had to prepare to leave. He had to set his dreams aside, as if he were casting flowers into darkness, a futile lover of the world whose desire always lacked courage.

He no longer had to regret having experienced nothing here. He did not even have to think about the past, just as he ignored the present and did not look to the future. He neither forgave nor loved. All that remained — apathy . . .

XXIII

Everything had failed. He was resigned to that. There was nothing more to be done. Everything in his life had withered even before he had tasted of anything. And suddenly his gardens were empty. The long inertia of dark hours had begun. Desire was extinguished, and no one came to visit anymore.

How had all this come to pass, how could it all have happened? Where before there had been a whole sea of life, now not even a drop remained. All destroyed — and in such a short time and forever! His entire *attempt at life* now seemed to him an effort to improvise on a violin whose strings had lost their sound and gone forever mute.

Now he huddled anxiously and submissively before the final blow, body and soul racked with nausea.

A melancholic withering away, prolonged, unending, or brief and silent madness? God, be merciful! he prayed. You are not an illusion, have mercy! Perhaps I have come too late, when belief is no longer possible. But do not punish me for the magnitude of that act. Forgive me for being too weak, for having dared deny You in myself...

Better not to think it through! To stop feeling! To fling cynical, radiant knowledge to the ground and shatter it! I'd rather have darkness than temptation and torment!

My eyes grew weary and could not see the storm. And the storm came and drowned me. My paths led through deep black forests, God, I could not recognize Your footprints — and I lost You. But You, God, who knows so many ways into the human soul, You, who takes another route when the first is barricaded: do not harden Your heart!

He awakened.

Where was he? Why was he kneeling?

He looked around. He was in the church of the Barnabites.

Such darkness everywhere. Darkness as in a tomb. Everywhere bleak shadows. And timid phantasms. Creeping along the walls. Sitting in the pews. Rising from the floor. Falling from the ceiling.

Suddenly the lights of a chandelier brightly flared up in the middle of the church. And the images above the altar came to life. And the fragrance of dead roses on the altars filled the air more pungently than long dead springs.

Then something very strange happened. In the back of the church a door opened, and a great and glorious procession entered — a procession of closely packed, indistinct figures with faces indistinguishable other than as a vague sense of something lighter trembling against an ever blacker background. Like Horror personified, those who had renounced life and buried their sighs in the dead walls of the cloister were entering the church.

The main altar blazed up again like an enormous *castrum doloris*. And again the oppressiveness of the Passion permeated the church, like the distressing atmosphere of funeral rites . . . Everything was just as it had been several years ago.

The huge Christ covered with bloody wounds, shining through the darkness as though aglow with mystical stigmata, now descended from the cross and walked slowly to the altar.

The nuns sat down in the pews. They bowed their heads and fell to their knees, agitated. They threw up their arms all at once, then dropped them, kissed the scapulary, then beat their breasts with penitent ardor.

Suddenly the sound of a small bell rang out by the altar. Christ, dressed in the chasuble of a priest, went up the steps and served Mass. A cloud of incense momentarily veiled his figure.

In the madness of ecstasy mingled with pain the penitents crawled up to Him, then nothing could be seen but a mass of bodies on the floor of the church. Above them He stood, the triumphant Victor, raising the paten with the host and the chalice with the sacred wine.

A wild, joyous singing erupted, singing of the greatest ecstasy of supreme gratitude, as if it were choking them but still had to push its way out, push its way out no matter what, even if its convulsions tore the whole body asunder. As if in their singing were a fanfare of all suppressed life and suppressed sexuality, as if it were beating against the walls of the church and demolishing them, raising the roof, and knocking out the windows and doors, sounding ever more jubilant and wild.

Now it was time for the triumphant trombones of the triumphant Song of Songs . . .

Yes, they live, they have not died; they live, even though they have renounced everything in life for Him. They have overcome His resistance through holy madness. Through their great, heroic renunciation they have mounted the stairs leading to His throne.

He now belongs to them. He will not escape them. They are connected to Him. They love His Silent Majesty, His endless, inexhaustible Power. And while Space and Time vanish, while everything around collapses and crashes down like waves into the depths of a whirlpool — He remains, and they with Him.

They don't even know where they are, who they are, whence they have come. They have forgotten their fathers and mothers. They have forgotten the names they had on Earth . . . They continuously sing to Him the same hymn, now older than millennia and more ancient than primeval times. And he feels how through them, their bodies, nerves, veins, bones, and all the fibers of their flesh, runs a single sensation of bliss, the unifying pain-pleasure of Mary and Magdalene, the mother holding the tortured naked body of the Son in her lap, and the sinner embracing the dead heavenly Lover and hiding his face in waves of luxuriant hair, unbound and saturated with ointments.

Again the bell sounded from the altar three times, and the nuns sang quietly and humbly, Sanctus, Sanctus, Sanctus . . .

All at once he cried out, he cried out so that He who was finishing the service of Mass by the altar would hear him, cried out with all his soul, wretched and reprobate, so that heaven would hear him, this heaven that had denied and abandoned him, repeating over and over, as loud as he could, in the silence, taking the breath away from everyone present, the strange, foreign words fixed in his memory:

— Eli, eli, lama sabachthani . . .

Then he burst into tears and beat his head against the ground.

XXIV

They led him from the church, where he had suddenly gone mad.

He was now completely silent. He only wept bitterly.

They took him to a mental institution. The doctors pronounced him incurable.

Because he had no relatives who could care for him, his house was sold.

The proceeds from the sale went to the institution. He lived there, miserable, in silent madness, for a few years before he died.

As he was dying he regained lucidity for a brief moment. He looked around and asked the nurse where he was.

When he received no response, he wanted to raise himself up on the bed to find out. But his dejected head collapsed back onto the hot pillows.

He then dreamed of a distant metropolis. He heard the sounds of its early evening, the trot of horses on the cobblestones, the rattling wheels of carriages, the irritable laughter of pedestrians. He saw the gaslights, casting reflections on the wet sidewalks.

He experienced everything once more. He saw the Powder Tower and the great bridge with its statues . . . He saw a funeral procession, and behind the coffin walked so many familiar faces. He recalled that man well: he was especially kind, for he always smiled at him when they met. That man: wasn't he the young, sick stranger he had seen on the train?

Oh, there were so many of them, so many, so many he knew and loved. And many who didn't live at all in this life. They visited him only when he dreamed of them at night. Oh, such beautiful faces, such delicate lips, such pale hands . . . How serene and happy they all were.

He called out a name.

The nurse stood up, but did not understand him.

The death-rattle began. Individual sounds merged, yet he had not lost consciousness entirely. He had awakened for a short time from such a long sleep. Was he now falling into an even longer sleep?

For a while he resisted this new extinction of his being. He also wanted to ask them to open the window curtain, for he would so like to see if it was day or night out . . .

He suddenly heaved a deep and painful sigh.

He knew that no one understood him any longer and that no one would come.

He died shortly before daybreak. For a moment there reigned one of those horrible silences that surround the bed of someone who has just passed away. But then the trees beneath the window began to rustle, as if shivering from the damp wind. And rain started to fall, silent and listless, sorrowful and melancholy . . .

LIST OF ILLUSTRATIONS

Wood engravings selected from an album published by J.J. Weber in Leipzig in 1896

TRANSLATOR'S AFTERWORD

Jiří Karásek's novella *A Gothic Soul* (1900), the most acclaimed Czech Decadent prose work both in its time and at present, expresses concerns that are unique to the Czech movement, while alluding creatively to "the breviary of the decadence," Joris-Karl Huysmans's *Against Nature* (1884). Karásek's often ironic play with this seminal text reveals profound differences between the Czech and French variants of the Decadent movement. In both works, the protagonist is the typical degenerate "last scion of a noble line" who retreats from the world. However, whereas Des Esseintes of *Against Nature* has led a life of extravagance from which he wishes to escape, Karásek's unnamed protagonist has never experienced anything and continues to yearn for life. More importantly, unlike Des Esseintes, he is also explicitly portrayed as an embodiment of his moribund nation: in Prague it seems "as though everything around him had already died out, and he too was but a part of that death." Prague is portrayed as a dead city peopled by shades, living, like the protagonist, only in the memory of its medieval splendor.

While Des Esseintes is a creator, Karásek's protagonist is a nihilist. Des Esseintes lavishly constructs his own world, whereas Karásek's considerably less wealthy protagonist merely ponders questions of religion and atheism, the vanity of life, his own sense of alienation, and the miserable situation of the Czechs. His retreat involves not the creation of an alternative world through material goods, but complete asceticism. He admires monasticism as "the only way to live life in a unified way." It is the epitome of the medieval way of life, which stands for unity and wholeness, as opposed to the alienation and fragmentation of contemporary society. He is drawn to Catholicism, but is ultimately, and tragically, unable to accept it. It is important to note, however, that Karásek avoids sentimentalism by treating his main character and his ideals with a measure of distancing irony and dark humor: the narrator states, for instance, that the protagonist thinks himself "an exceptional, medieval soul" since he is "so ecstatically enamored of mold and putrefaction." At times the novella, composed over a decade after the emergence of Decadence in the Czech lands, parodies stereotypical Decadent motifs.

The main character comes to understand that the renunciation of life is meaningless unless one has already experienced it to the full. This is the lesson he derives from a painting of Mary Magdalene, which he describes with allusions to Huysmans's famed ekphrasis of Gustave Moreau's *Salomé*. Karásek's Mary, however, is not Huysmans's "symbolic deity of indestructible Lechery."* Although her eyes gleam with

* J.-K. Huysmans, *Against Nature,* tr. Margaret Mauldon (Oxford, 1998), 46.

sensuality, she does not gloat triumphantly over the head of John the Baptist; instead, she repents sorrowfully over a skull, symbol of the vanity of life. The narrator evokes her past in terms reminiscent of Huysmans's Salomé: she once lived in "an atmosphere of thrilling vice," an atmosphere of "pleasure, laughter, dance, [and] rousing nakedness." She has experienced all pleasures and all sins, followed by "repulsion and exhaustion." Only then could she devote herself to Christ. The vacillating protagonist doubts the value of this dedication, however, as he sees despair in her pose and death in the pallid glow of her body.

It is death that dominates Karásek's "flower scene" as well. Des Esseintes's flower collection reflects his fear of sexuality, and particularly of syphilis. Karásek's protagonist associates his own much more modest collection, which consists only of roses and tuberoses, mainly with death. He prefers his tuberoses, which are "as pale as the forehead of a dying man, enfeebled in their flaccidity, vanquished by their own breath, mournful, sanctified by death." Absorbed in the fragrance of these flowers, he dreams of "the sweet and painless death of the depressed and listless." He often longs for such a death, and, in contrast to *Against Nature,* Karásek's novella indeed ends with the protagonist's madness and demise. As Karásek phrases it in the Preface, it is "the impossibility of faith," as well as the impossibility of escaping from himself, that has led to his destruction.

The protagonists of both works interrupt their suffocating solitude with a journey by train, and in both cases the trip is cut short. Des Esseintes ultimately finds that his conception of his destinations — London and Holland — based on literature are more satisfying than the places themselves, and he would rather travel in his imagination than put up with all of the inconveniences of actual travel. Karásek's protagonist's trip is very different: he has no destination, but is seeking a passionate friendship that consists in "the union of two bodies as well as the union of two souls." He hungers for a male companion.

For Karásek the theme of homosexuality was not only personal: he integrated it into the very paradigm of Decadence by associating it with degeneration, a central preoccupation of the movement. According to degeneration theorists, modern society was sick because the environment necessary for natural selection had halted evolution, and conditions such as the growth of cities and alcoholism had set the stage for degeneration or evolutionary regression, which had become hereditary. Homosexuality and tuberculosis were widely viewed as symptoms of degeneration. Karásek unites these conditions in his protagonist's meeting with a young man in the train. Coughing racks the youth, and his illness has imbued his lips with a deep red. His cheeks have "the tinge of roses starting to wither," and his intelligent face reveals profound suffering. At the same time, his behavior and dress suggest a noble birth, and Karásek's protagonist chooses the name of a count's family in the region that sounds proud and glorious, and he imagines the young man to be the last scion of that family. He wonders whether that man, with whom he cannot bring himself to speak, could be the intimate friend he has been seeking. Karásek thus not only links homosexuality with degeneration insofar as the object of desire is dying of tuberculosis, he also implies that the homosexual is a quintessential Decadent — the last scion of a noble line. In addition, the man's bloody lips evoke the image of the vampire, a common symbol throughout Karásek's fiction. The vampire represents for Karásek the craving of the homosexual who cannot satisfy a need as vital as the vampire's need for blood. The vampire also represents the dying Czech nation, which cannot satisfy its need for life — for community — in contemporary society.

If the Czech Decadents are satiated, it is only with their frustrated longings for change and with the Baroque nothingness that Karásek emphasizes throughout *A Gothic Soul*. Despair and death are dominant motifs of Western Decadence, but in Czech Decadence they become obsessions, at least in part because of the Decadents' concern for the fate of their nation. It is only in the Czech lands that the motifs of futility and fatalism both predominate and arise directly from the political situation. Moreover, because the chief representative of Czech Decadence, following Oscar Wilde, openly expresses his same-sex desires and incorporates them into the framework of Decadence, homosexuality is not merely alluded to — as in *Against Nature* — it is a crucial element of the Czech movement. The protagonist of *A Gothic Soul* hungers for spiritual meaning, for the unity of his nation, and for a special friend, but ultimately all of his desires are thwarted.

Kirsten Lodge
2015

JIŘÍ KARÁSEK (ZE LVOVIC)

Under the auspices of the Decadent journal *The Modern Revue* (*Moderní revue*), founded in October 1894 by Arnošt Procházka and Jiří Karásesk, Decadence flourished in the Czech lands more than anywhere else in Central and Eastern Europe. The journal was modeled on the leading French Decadent-Symbolist journal *Mercure de France* and journals edited by Anatole Baju, particularly *Le Décadent*. Yet the movement's themes of despair, impotence, and frustration found especial resonance among the Czechs, who had been striving in vain for decades to gain greater rights within the Austro-Hungarian Empire. Procházka and Karásek edited *The Modern Revue*, the most significant and widely known Czech modernist journal, until Procházka's death in 1925, and the two headed the Decadent movement, with Procházka writing chiefly manifestos, reviews, and theoretical and polemical essays promoting the new movement, and Karásek publishing Decadent poetry, drama, and prose as well as non-fiction, including criticism, polemics, and theoretical essays. Karásek continued to devote himself to Decadent themes through the 1920s, well after the movement had waned elsewhere. He was by far the most prolific Czech Decadent writer, and is generally held to be the most interesting.

Karásek (later known by the pseudonym Karásek ze Lvovic) was born on January 24, 1871, into a poor family in Prague. He was fascinated by death and decay from a young age, and these Decadent themes naturally became integral to his fiction. Several of his siblings died in childhood, and in his memoirs he writes that he used to visit their graves in the Mála Strana (Lesser Town) Cemetery to commune with their souls. His father also died suddenly in 1890. Karásek completed high school and began to study theology at Charles University in Prague, but soon dropped out, doubting his vocation as a Catholic priest. He then decided to become a teacher, but lacked the financial resources necessary to complete the requisite studies. Regretting that he could not devote himself entirely to literature, in 1892 he became a civil servant in the postal service. In 1896, he was promoted to Imperial and Royal postal assistant, and in 1921 he became the director of the Postal Museum and Archives, retiring in 1933. Like T.S. Eliot, Franz Kafka, and Joris-Karl Huysmans, Karásek worked in a full-time professional clerical position while devoting all of his free time to literature.

While a lack of resources and the consequent inability to become a full-time writer, or at least work in a more fulfilling capacity, were frustrating, the sense of despair that is so prevalent in Karásek's fiction stemmed in large part from his homosexuality. The same-sex desire he experienced was shunned by the society of his day, which had laws that criminalized homosexual acts. Karásek kept his sexual orientation to himself until he courageously published the first collection of openly homoerotic poetry in 1895, *Sodom*, which came out in connection with his journal's intrepid defense of Oscar Wilde, then on trial for committing homosexual acts. *Sodom* was confiscated and destroyed by the authorities. Karásek was investigated by the police, but not charged with any crime. A later trilogy, *Novels of Three Magi* (1907, 1908, 1925), features erudite homosexual characters steeped in the occult sciences, inspired by the stories of magic and alchemy surrounding Holy Roman Emperor and King of Bohemia Rudolf II. Karásek became as well one of the first political defenders of homosexuality in the early twentieth century.

Karásek began to study French language and literature in 1884, when his schoolmate Procházka introduced him to the French Naturalists and Symbolists. Karásek started with Émile Zola and his Naturalist school and the critics Paul Bourget and Hippolyte Taine, soon discovering Charles Baudelaire, Paul Verlaine, Henryk Ibsen, Victor Hugo, and Anatole France. In July 1892, he made his literary debut with a critical article on Walt Whitman, followed by articles on German modernism. He first encountered the work of the Polish writer Stanisław Przybyszewski, whom he considered a model Decadent, in 1893, and the experience left him astounded. Procházka and Karásek soon began to collaborate with Przybyszewski, who was based in Berlin and had close associations with German and Scandinavian modernists, including the artist Edvard Munch. Returning to Krakow in 1898, Przybyszewski became the editor of the Polish avant-garde journal *Życie* (*Life*) and established a close working relationship between the Czech and Polish avant-gardes.

Starting in 1896, Karásek's new position with the postal service required him to travel regularly to Vienna. According to his memoirs, he met a very cultured young count there, a diplomat, with whom he fell in love. Karásek describes his lover as an aristocrat descended from Czech nobility and resembling Des Esseintes of Huysmans's *Against Nature*, and he notes that this friend introduced him to many Viennese noblemen and writers, including Hugo von Hofmannsthal. Inspired by Viennese salons, Karásek began to dress as a dandy, and Procházka soon followed suit. Karásek credited his lover with encouraging him to expand his art collection, which he had begun in 1893, and he gradually acquired a large number of works, supplemented by gifts and donations. He opened his collection to the public in 1924.

Karásek's popularity began to wane as new movements gradually took the place of Decadence after the turn of the century. Nevertheless, he continued to write prolifically throughout the 1920s and build up his art collection, which became one of the largest in Europe. He was increasingly drawn to Catholicism, and many of his later works may be described as Catholic legends with Decadent elements. He even co-edited a Catholic literary journal from 1918 to 1921. The occult also figures prominently in his later work, and he edited an occultist journal from 1923 to 1925. In 1921, he was promoted to the post of director of the Postal and Communications Ministry and began to collect materials for the Postal Museum. Retiring in 1933, he published little until his death in 1951. He is buried in Prague's Malvazinka Cemetery.

K.L.

ABOUT THE TRANSLATOR

Kirsten Lodge is Assistant Professor of English and Humanities and Humanities Program Coordinator at Midwestern State University. Her books include: *Translating the Early Poetry of Velimir Khlebnikov*; *Solitude, Vanity, Night: An Anthology of Czech Decadent Poetry*; *The Dedalus Book of Russian Decadence: Perversity, Despair, and Collapse*; and new translations of Dostoevsky's *Notes from the Underground* and Leo Tolstoy's *The Death of Ivan Ilyich*.

ABOUT THE ARTIST

Sascha Schneider (1870–1927) was born in St. Petersburg and lived much of his life in Germany, where he studied art in Dresden and taught at the Saxon-Grand Ducal Art School. His great inspiration was the Symbolist artist Max Klinger, whose work he recast into his own original conception of Decadence often with homosexual overtones.

A Gothic Soul by Jiří Karásek ze Lvovic
is translated by Kirsten Lodge from the original Czech
Gotická duše, first published in 1900 by Moderní revue in Prague

Artwork by Sascha Schneider
Cover concept by Dan Mayer
Text set in Garamond Premier Pro by Silk Mountain

We are indebted to Pavel Růt for sharing his collection of Sascha Schneider prints and preparing the reproductions

FIRST SOFTCOVER EDITION 2025

First published in hardcover in 2015

TWISTED SPOON PRESS
P.O. Box 21 – Preslova 12
150 00 Prague 5
Czech Republic
www.twistedspoon.com

Printed and bound in Poland by Books Factory

Distributed to the trade by
CENTRAL BOOKS
www.centralbooks.com

SCB DISTRIBUTORS
www.scbdistributors.com